LAW OF THE GUN

BRETT RIDER

SAGEBRUSH
Large Print Westerns

First published in Great Britain by ISIS Publishing
First published in the United States by Macrae Smith

Published in Large Print 2011 by ISIS Publishing Ltd.,
7 Centremead, Osney Mead, Oxford OX2 0ES
United Kingdom
by arrangement with
Golden West Literary Agency

All rights reserved

The moral right of the author has been asserted

British Library Cataloguing in Publication Data
Rider, Brett, 1879–1971.
    Law of the gun.
    1. Western stories.
    2. Large type books.
    I. Title
    813.5'2–dc22

ISBN 978–0–7531–8746–3 (pb)

Printed and bound in Great Britain by
T. J. International Ltd., Padstow, Cornwall

CHAPTER
ONE

The Night Stage

The evening shadows crawled up the street and darkened the hotel lobby, touching the beginnings of a frown on Sam Doan's face. With an impatient glance at the door, he got out of the chair behind the desk and went to the big swing kerosene lamp.

He glowered at it for a moment, then snagged the draw chain with the steel hook he used in place of a hand. The shank of the hook was tightly wrapped with rawhide worn and polished to the color of old saddle leather.

He jerked the lamp down, scraped a sulphur match against trouser leg, and touched the flame to the round wick, waited for the flicker to settle to an even glow, and carefully pulled on the chain until the lamp was again in position.

Annoyance grew in him as he stood there. Lighting the lamp was a chore he disliked. Pete Walker, his night clerk, was supposed to show up at sundown and attend to it. Pete had been getting in late from supper for the past week, and it was Sam's shrewd guess that he was sweet on the little blonde waitress at the Home Café.

Sam's frown deepened. He was a solid-built man in his early sixties, and had grown a paunch since he had given up his job as foreman of the Flying Y outfit to become owner of the San Lucas Hotel. He was thinking that Pete was old enough to know better than make eyes at a chit of a girl. They didn't come finer than Pete, but he had always been soft in the head when it came to pert-faced females.

Sam turned in a speculative look at the three men who sat at a small table near the stairs that rose steeply to the second floor. Two of them were strangers, soft-spoken, calm-eyed. He sized them up for cowmen. The third of the trio, tall, lean, gray-haired, was his former boss, Ed Yate, owner of the Flying Y ranch and, like his companions, he carried a gun in low-slung holster. A circumstance that made Sam wonder. Ed Yate seldom wore a gun.

They were waiting for the overdue stage from Deming, and killing time with a desultory game of poker, pausing often to engage in low-voiced conversation that even Sam's lynx-sharp ears had been unable to overhear. He guessed that they had more important matters than cards on their minds.

The Flying Y man met his thoughtful look. "Thanks for the light, Sam," he drawled. "Wasn't sure I was holdin' a full house or just five no-good cards."

Sam gave him a skeptical grin. "It ain't *cards* that's on your mind, Ed," he said. His look shifted expectantly to the door. "Sounds like Pete."

The night clerk, a lean, wiry little man, hurried in from the porch, a placating grin on his leathery face.

Like Sam Doan, he was a former Flying Y man and walked with a slight limp, a memento of the same stampede that had cost Sam his right hand and ended their riding days.

He slid behind the desk, thumbed over a page of the register and sent another grin at his reproachful boss.

"Stage comin'," he announced. "I reckon Andy Sims figgers to make up some lost time the way he's hittin' the downgrade."

Cards spilled on the table near the stairs, chairs scraped, and in a moment Ed Yate and his two companions were on the run to the door.

Sam Doan's gaze followed them into the growing dusk outside. He pushed up the battered Stetson he was seldom seen without, and thoughtfully fingered his grizzled mustache. He could have sworn he had glimpsed a bright glint of metal under the coat of the smaller of Ed Yate's companions. The man was a law officer.

Sam was deeply puzzled, uneasy. His alert mind told him that some desperate business was in the making. He was inclined to feel hurt at the way Ed Yate was keeping his mouth shut about it. Ed was his old-time boss, one of the most prominent cowmen in the Territory of New Mexico and head of the recently organized San Lucas Stockmen's Association. He resented Ed's apparent attempt to keep him in the dark about the business that had brought the mysterious strangers to meet the stage from Deming.

He could hear the stage rattling across Dry Creek at the foot of the grade, the drumming hoofs of Andy's

3

six-horse hitch. Andy was pouring leather. It irked the old stage driver to bring the mail in late.

Sam's gaze returned to Pete who was fitting a fresh pen into the thick wooden holder. "What do you make of them two fellers with Ed?" he asked.

Pete placed the pen near the bottle of ink, shook his head. "All I savvy about 'em is the names they wrote down here in the register." He thumbed back a page, narrowed his eyes. "One of 'em sets it down he's from Santa Fe, name of A. B. Holcomb — he's the little feller. The other hombre claims to come from Silver City, name of J. O. Barr." Pete narrowed his eyes thoughtfully. "I reckon he's the feller that owns that big JO Bar spread, on the Gila."

"You ain't tellin' me nothin'," grumbled Sam. "I got eyes and can read. I was askin' what you *make* of 'em."

"You can read brand as good as I can," Pete told him huffily. "Why don't you ask Ed Yate?"

Sam grinned. "You know the way Ed is. He don't answer questions 'less he's a mind to."

"That's right," agreed Pete. "Ed gets lockjaw awful quick when he don't figger to talk."

Sam's frown returned. He gave Pete a piercing look. "You watch yourself with that yeller head over to the Home Café," he said heavily. "First thing you know she'll have you roped an' tied for keeps."

Pete grinned. "Jealous, huh?" He rubbed a fresh-shaved cheek complacently. "She's a right smart-lookin' heifer, I'm tellin' you."

"You poor old mossyhorn!" The affection in Sam's voice belied the jibe. The friendship between these two men was deep and abiding. Sam would have lost more than a hand in that stampede if Pete Walker had not stopped to pull him from under his dead horse. The affair had left Pete with a broken leg and a limp that would be with him for the rest of his days.

Sam turned to the door. "Reckon I'll ramble over to the post office," he said. "Like as not Andy's fetched us some mail. The *Republican* is due in today from Santa Fe."

Pete's skeptical grin followed him into the fast fading twilight. He was not fooled by Sam's talk about the mail. Sam smelled excitement, and his curiosity was running full.

Sam found the usual crowd gathered on the wide porch of Joe Slocum's General Merchandise Store a short block down the street from the hotel. Joe was postmaster, a lanky man with frosted black hair and cynical eyes in a lined, brown face. Nothing ever seemed to disturb his equanimity, not even a long unpaid bill. He stood there on the high porch, under the flare of two big swing lamps, patient gaze on the stage rattling up the street.

"More'n an hour late," he said to Sam, as the hotel man climbed the steps. "Seems like all the folks in town is waitin' for their mail. Have to wait some more before I get the pouch sorted."

Sam nodded. "Some folks is always lookin' for mail they don't get," he chuckled. His roving gaze fastened on Ed Yate and the pair of strangers who were down in the street, slightly behind the big store and just beyond the revealing lamplight. From where they stood they

5

would have an unobstructed view of the passengers when they climbed from the stage.

Joe Slocum spoke softly, "Looks like Vince Lestang is expectin' somebody in on the stage."

Sam's look went to the man approaching from across the street. The light from the swing lamps showed a handsome face, dark, sardonic, a flash of white teeth under the waxed black mustache. He wore an immaculate white Stetson hat and a double-breasted black coat open to reveal a strawberry-red waistcoat.

"That doggone dandy sticks in my craw," growled Sam.

"Vince Lestang is makin' pots of money in this cow town," Joe Slocum said. "His Border Palace Bar is a gold mine, and he's doin' a right smart business buyin' and sellin' cattle and land." The storekeeper frowned, lowered his voice. "Vince is gettin' so big, he about runs this town."

Sam was silent. He was wondering if Vince Lestang also was expecting excitement when the stage pulled in. The saloon man usually sent over for his mail.

The big Concord rocked up, old Andy Sims hunched forward on his high seat, his customary grin absent. He jammed on the brakes, brought the stage to a standstill alongside the platform. Dust drifted past and Sam heard Andy's aggrieved voice.

"Got held up by a boulder layin' plumb acrost the road in Red Cliff Canyon," he told Joe Slocum. "Had to git chains and tie onto it with the team. Took more'n an hour." He reached under his feet, dragged out the mail bag. "Here she is, Joe." He heaved the pouch to the platform, and turned his attention to his passengers.

The passenger list was short; a lean, whiskered prospector, a couple of cavalrymen from Fort Bayard, a bandy-legged cowboy, followed by a too-elegantly dressed blonde girl who held her face disdainfully away from the broadside of interested looks, a hand daintily holding long skirts from the dust.

Sam Doan's surmises about the business that had brought Vince Lestang to meet the stage were quickly settled. The tall saloon man was instantly at the girl's side. He spoke to her softly, beckoned a Mexican to shoulder the small leather trunk Andy Sims dragged from the boot. It was obvious that Lestang's Border Palace was to have an added attraction.

Sam's gaze now fastened on the last passenger to climb from the stage, and something vaguely familiar about the man sharpened his attention.

He was young, of medium height, lean and sinewy as a panther, and the glare of the lamps full on him showed dark hair, a pleasant, boyish face. He wore the plain, serviceable garb of a cowman and, for all his seeming youth, there was something formidable about him, an air of quiet efficiency.

Ed Yate and his two companions were suddenly closing in, their guns out, and Sam heard Yate's voice, a hard, chill sound that put a hush on the crowd there.

"Keep your hand away from that gun!"

The young man eyed him up and down, looked at the other two, the boyishness gone from him now. He

7

suddenly seemed years older, his face hard, his eyes wary.

"Who's telling me?" He put the question softly, hand poised over gun butt, like a hawk ready to swoop.

"We'll save the talk until we get you into a jail cell," the Fying Y man said curtly. He gestured at the smaller of his two companions. "This is U. S. Deputy Marshal Holcomb."

Holcomb waggled his gun. "Get your hands up fast. You're under arrest."

A buckboard rattled into the street, came to a quick halt. The driver, an elderly rancher, muttered an ejaculation.

"Looks like that feller's in trouble, Mary," he said to the girl by his side.

The young man, his hands up now, met her wondering look. She averted her gaze quickly, and something like dismay momentarily shadowed his face, or it might have been shame.

He spoke softly to the deputy marshal. "What's the charge?"

"Cattle rustling," rasped Holcomb.

"You've got the wrong man."

"Your name's Malory, ain't it?" demanded the deputy marshal.

"That's right," admitted the young man. "Kingman Malory."

"Also known as *King* Malory." Holcomb spoke in a loud, blustering voice. It was apparent he wanted the crowd to hear his words. "King Malory," he repeated, "outlaw, border smuggler."

Young Malory was silent. He seemed worried, looked again at the sea of faces, this time appealingly. Sam caught an impatient gesture from Vince Lestang, watching from the street, the blonde girl's hand on his arm.

"Somebody is crazy." The saloon man's voice was contemptuous, edged with anger. "That kid is no outlaw!"

Ed Yate's look reached to him. "Keep out of this business, Vince." His tone was grim. "We don't need your ideas about it."

Lestang shrugged an elegant shoulder. "Come on, Estelle," he said to the girl. "I reckon he's right at that." They went on across the street.

Holcomb spoke again. "Know this man?" He gestured at his taller companion.

His prisoner made no attempt to look. "Take me over to your jail," he said. "I'm done with talking."

"He owns the JO Bar ranch down on the Gila. He claims you've rustled him to the bone."

"I'm done with talking," repeated King Malory.

"Barr has been on your trail for months," continued Holcomb. "He's got proof that'll send you to prison, maybe swing you for murder."

Ed Yate glanced uneasily at the crowd, said curtly to Holcomb, "Let's get him over to the jail. We're wasting time."

King Malory gave him a bitter smile. "I'm only hoping your jail isn't as dirty as some I've had a look at." His glance went briefly to the girl in the buckboard as he turned away, Holcomb's gun at his back.

Her gaze followed him, and the pity was plain enough now in her eyes. Her companion muttered something, touched the team with his whip, and they drove on past the store toward the livery barn at the end of the street.

Sam Doan's gaze also followed the prisoner, an incredulous look on his rugged face. Heedless of the excited, pushing crowd, he stood there, memories stirring in him of the days of his lusty youth when the southwest was one vast free range.

A picture shaped, the bawling trail-herd, the dread *Jornado del Muerto* — the Horsehead crossing on the Pecos and thirst-maddened cattle stampeding into the river, himself trapped in the rush, fighting for his life in the muddy, swift-flowing current, his horse drowning under him.

Sam suddenly slapped a still hard thigh. Memory burned bright now. "*Must be!*" he muttered. "The spittin' image of him." His frown deepened. "Cain't figger this business. Somethin' is awful wrong."

His face a thundercloud, he pushed into the big store, elbowed his way to the little window where Joe Slocum was handing out the mail.

Joe shoved a folded newspaper at him. "No letters, Sam." There was a gleam in his cynical eyes. "Looks like Ed Yate's new Association means business," he drawled.

Sam scowled, grunted, turned away with his newspaper. He was feeling a bit sick. Something was wrong, and what to do about it had him puzzled. He was wanting a heart-to-heart talk with Ed Yate.

CHAPTER
TWO

Sam Doan Remembers

Sam went thoughtfully back to the hotel. Pete Walker had lighted the big porch lamp and was standing in the doorway, an annoyed look on his face as he watched two young cowboys push through the screen door of the Home Café. He gave Sam a gloomy look.

"Them Flyin' Y fellers give me a pain in the stummick," he grumbled. "Jest cain't keep away from that place."

"Jealous as an old range bull, huh," growled Sam unsympathetically. "Quit pawin' dust over that blonde heifer." He gestured impatiently. "Come back to the desk. We got more important things to talk about."

The harsh rasp in his voice drew a penetrating look from Pete. He nodded, limped to the desk, leaned on it while Sam lowered his heavy frame into the chair.

"What's on your mind?" he asked. "You sure look red-eyed."

Sam was unfolding his newspaper, the Santa Fe *Republican*, smoothing it out with the hook he used for a right hand, and Pete, watching him, wondered at the curious expression on his old friend's face. He read horror there, a blending of grief and hot anger.

"What the heck's wrong, Sam?" He took two quick steps, peered over Sam's shoulder at the spread-out newspaper.

"*That's* wrong!" Sam spoke hoarsely. "Damn wrong!" His voice was suddenly a groan. "*It ain't possible!*"

"Take your big thumb off the pitcher," grumbled Pete. "Cain't see the feller's pitcher for your thumb layin' on it."

Sam's hand slid aside. Pete stared at the picture of a slim, cool-eyed youth. He gave Sam a puzzled look.

"Ain't knowin' him a-tall," he said.

"Read what it says about him." Sam touched the caption with his steel hook. "He's the young feller Ed Yate and those fellers took off the stage. They've throwed him in jail."

Pete narrowed his eyes, lips moving soundlessly as he read.

"This piece says the feller's name is King Malory," he said. "Claims he's sure one bad man."

"A damn lie!" snorted Sam.

"Says he's boss of a border gang of rustlers that's got the cowmen of the southwest crazy." Pete muttered a startled exclamation. "It says here that J. O. Barr, biggest cattleman in Grant County and chief victim of the notorious outlaw's gang, has learned that King Malory has fled to the San Lucas country and that plans are being made to apprehend him." Pete's finger went back to the name of J. O. Barr. "That's the feller that's registered from Silver City," he said.

"Sure is," grunted Sam. "The other feller is a U. S. deputy marshal, doggone Ed Yate's hide."

Pete went back to the side of the desk, stared curiously at him. "How come you got so on the prod about them throwin' this young feller in jail? He's one bad hombre, from what this piece in the paper says."

There was reproach in Sam's eyes. "You keep your mind so set on blondes you ain't got memory for nothin'." He scratched a beetling nose with the sharp point of his hook. "Don't the name of King Malory mean somethin' to you?"

Pete muttered a startled exclamation and he was silent for a long moment, a faraway expression in his sun-wrinkled eyes. "*King Malory!*" He spoke softly, a deep awe in his voice. "Me an' you was with him the time he fetched that bunch of cows across the *Jornado del Muerto*." Pete shook his head. "Mighty lot of years ago, Sam, when we signed on with King Malory to prod them longhorns across that backyard of hell. More'n forty years, I reckon."

"We was kids," Sam Doan said. His eyes were bright, warmed by stirring and fond memories. "King Malory showed us how to be growed men — taught us all there was to know about cows." He paused, added softly, "He saved my life that time at Horsehead crossing. I was drownin' when he clamped hold of me, dragged me to the bank."

"They never come better no time than old King Malory," Pete Walker said. He shook his head sadly. "Never seemed right, danglin' him for a cow thief the way they done."

Sam Doan clenched his huge left hand. "It was murder, Pete." He spoke solemnly, his voice hardly more than a hoarse whisper. "Me an' you wasn't never able to prove it, an' we couldn't do nothin'. Had to see him swing at the end of a rope."

Pete Walker reached inside a drawer of the desk, fished out a dark plug of tobacco. He gnawed off a chew, replaced the tobacco in the drawer, slammed it shut with a bang. His hand was not quite steady.

He said, softly, "I'm gettin' the pitcher, Sam." He gestured at the crumpled newspaper lying across the other man's knees. "You figger this young feller is old King's boy, huh?"

"Looks like him, the same as two peas in a pod." Sam straightened up in the creaky chair. "Some younger than old King was when we knowed him — too young to be his son, but I'm betting he's a grandson, and he wears the same name."

"Never knowed King had a son some place. King wasn't much on talk about himself." He sent a dark brown stream into the brass spittoon that stood alongside the desk, added cryptically, "It was Cole Garson got him swung for a cow thief."

There was a long silence, the two men staring at each other, their thoughts churning. Noises came from the darkness beyond the door, the hammering hoofs of horses, shrill, joyful yells from their riders.

"Reckon that's the Bar G bunch," guessed Pete. He scowled. "That no-good Garson outfit sure make plenty hell when they hit town. Won't one of 'em be sober when they come in yellin' for rooms."

"I hate them rannies bunkin' down in this hotel," grumbled Sam.

"Cain't turn 'em away," reminded Pete. He shrugged. "We're here to accommodate the public, an' we sure need all the dollars we can get for our rooms."

Another long silence, broken by Sam. He said slowly, thoughtfully, "Cole Garson's been settin' pretty ever since he got old King out of the way."

Pete nodded, an angry glint in his eyes. "Never could savvy how come him and King got to be pardners in that spread." He shook his head. "Don't seem natcheral for a buzzard like him to mate up with a lion."

"Nobody knowed he was King's pardner until King was hung," Sam reminded. "Cole was runnin' a law office. It wasn't until after King was dead that Cole Garson flashed them papers making him sole owner of King's Circle M ranch."

"Always figgered that business smelled awful bad," muttered Pete. "I reckon you're right, Sam, claimin' old King was murdered."

Sam Doan heaved himself from the chair. "We got to do somethin' about it," he said grimly.

"No savvy." Pete was puzzled. "King's been dead close on fifteen years. Cain't see what we can do *now*."

Sam was glowering at the newspaper he held in his hand. He tapped it with his steel hook. "I'm talkin' about this young feller that wears the name of King Malory, him Ed Yate has got throwed in jail. I'm gamblin' my last chip he's some kin to old King, and that means he ain't no cow stealin' outlaw like this paper says."

15

"Ain't nothin' we can do about it," worried Pete.

"Old King was our friend," argued Sam. "We cain't set idle and see 'em pull off another smelly deal on this young feller that mebbe's his grandson."

"They got him in jail," reminded Pete. "Ed Yate helped put him there. We cain't buck a big man like Ed Yate."

Sam shook his head like an angry bull. "We ain't lettin' old King down ag'in," he declared. "Shake the moss off your horns, old-timer. You're goin' to want 'em plenty sharp."

"Huh?" Pete eyed him suspiciously. "What's buzzin' in your haid now?"

"Me and you is goin' to break the young feller out of that jail," Sam told him.

Pete pursed his lips in a soundless whistle, rubbed his chin thoughtfully.

"We owe it to old King to side this young maverick that wears his name," Sam said.

Pete heaved a deep sigh, nodded. "Reckon that's right, Sam. I'm backin' your play and there ain't no limit." His eyes were suddenly bright. "Sure crave some excitement for a change. Gets awful dull, settin' here at this doggone desk." He reached for his hat. "I'll chase over to Willie Logan's shack and tell him he's hired to ride night herd on things here."

Sam nodded agreement. "Been thinkin' of puttin' Willie on reg'lar," he said.

"Fixin' to fire me, huh?" exclaimed Pete.

"Fixin' to make you pardners with me in this doggone place," grinned his old friend. "Me an' you

16

has rode stirrup to stirrup a lot of years, old-timer. Time you took it more easy."

A slow smile spread over Pete's leathery features. "You old son-of-a-gun." He spoke huskily, "Pardners, huh?" He broke off, choked, spat out his quid of tobacco. "Purty near swallered my chew," he spluttered.

Sam grinned at him, not for a moment deceived by Pete's attempt to cover his emotion. "We got to work fast," he said. "You hightail it over to Willie Logan and get him over here on the jump."

"He'll come, you bet your life," chuckled Pete. "Willie figgers to own the San Lucas Hotel one of these days. Never seen a feller so set on bein' a hotel man."

The creak of the screen door drew their attention, and Sam said genially, "Hello, folks. Seen you drivin' up the street and figgered you'd mebbe drop in."

The newcomers, a tall, elderly man and a young girl approached the desk.

"Ain't seen you in town for a coon's age," Sam continued. "How's things with you, Jim?"

"Mighty tough," Jim Carroll told him gloomily. He leaned over the dog-eared register, picked up the pen, dabbed it on the ink bottle. His dusty face wore an harassed look.

The girl, slim and supple, turned her head in a sharp look back at the door. A man's tall shape moved across the lamplit porch. The girl quickly averted her face, and the screen door creaked again and the man came into the lobby, stood looking at her.

Sam spoke again, and this time there was no warmth in his voice.

17

"Figgerin' to bunk your boys here tonight, Dal?"

"Six of us," the man said. He approached, a hint of a swagger in him, and his eyes, insolent, confident, finally drew the girl's look. "Hello, Mary." His smile was on her now, admiring, possessive. "Sure is good to see you."

Her response was brief, unsmiling. "How do you do, Mr. Santeen." She turned away, gave him her back again, and spoke to Sam Doan.

"We want to see Ed Yate, ask him to let us have the use of his Tecolote Canyon Springs."

Sam shook his head. "The Tecolote Springs is dry as last year's bones," he told her.

Jim Carroll flung down the pen, turned from the desk. "I'm sure up against it, Sam." His tone was despairing. "Every creek and spring on my range is dry, and my cows dying for water."

Sam was silent for a moment, speculative gaze on Santeen. "You could ask Dal here about Mesquite Springs," he suggested. "Plenty water at Mesquite Springs."

"Means a long drive," Carroll objected. "Ain't sure I can get 'em so far."

"How about it, Dal?" Sam was watching the tall Bar G foreman.

Santeen hesitated, sultry gaze still on Mary Carroll. It was plain that he was not liking the girl's disdain of him.

"I reckon the boss ain't lettin' nobody use Mesquite Springs." His tone was sulky. "We've throwed up a fence there, posted guards." He flung the girl an angry look, strode away to the door, paused there, glanced back at them. "Keep your cows away from the springs, Carroll, or you'll run into plenty trouble." The screen door slammed.

"The skunk," muttered Pete Walker. He shook his head. "He's right at that. Garson ain't lettin' nobody use that water."

"I'll use it, by God!" exploded Jim Carroll. "I'll water my cows there." He gestured despairingly. "Providin' I can get 'em that far."

Sam's frown was on Pete, and he said curtly, "You go tell Willie Logan to come on the jump."

Pete said, "Sure." He limped into the darkness.

Sam's compassionate look was on the girl. "You seem mighty tired, Mary. Et your supper yet?"

"Yes." Mary Carroll smiled at him, golden brown eyes warm as she met his kindly look. "We stopped in at the Home Café." She paused, added worriedly, "We saw them arrest that boy."

"Yeah." Sam looked uncomfortable. "Seen you drive up."

"He didn't look like a bandit," Mary said.

"Mebbe he ain't," Sam said briefly.

"I felt, well, sorry for him." Mary frowned. "I suppose I'm just foolish. Too tired to think straight."

Her father said wearily, "That's right, Sam. I reckon she's plumb wore out, ridin' over this damn country with me lookin' for some place we can get water for the herd." He clenched big fists. "Looks like this two year drought is goin' to ruin me, Sam. If we don't get the herd to water awful quick it's going to finish the JC for keeps."

Sam said gruffly, "You quit worryin', Jim. Best thing you and Mary can do is to hit the hay." He forced a grin. "Tomorrow's another day, huh?"

"Want Mary to get some rest," the JC man said wearily. "Got to be ridin' come midnight and head back to the ranch." The cattleman's face darkened. "I'm pushing the herd to Mesquite Springs, and to hell with Cole Garson and his barbed-wire fence."

Sam's look went to the girl, and the pity in his eyes seemed to lift her chin still higher. Her smile came again, the dimple in her cheek in no way lessening its defiance.

"If we can get the herd to Mesquite Springs we are going to water them," she said. "No range hog is going to stop us."

"That's fightin' talk," Sam said. His eyes approved her, smiled encouragement. "You go get some sleep, Mary. Room 7, right down the hall, is all fixed. Your pa will have the room next to you. Don't want you goin' upstairs. Bunch of fellers in town will be up there."

"That Bar G outfit," Jim Carroll said sourly.

"Reckon you'll be headin' for the ranch, time they get in," Sam said. "Ain't takin' chances at that, so you and Mary go bunk in them rooms down the hall. Keep 'em for decent folks."

He stood there by the desk, steel hook thoughtfully fingering his grizzled hair. "It's likely me and Pete won't be in the office. Got some business to 'tend to."

Mary's father nodded. "Come on, Mary," he said, and with a curt gesture he crossed the lobby to the hall door.

Sam watched them until the closing door shut them from view. His look lowered to the crumpled newspaper. The story there was a lie. Cow thieves did not spring from old King Malory's breed.

He thought miserably of the tragedy that had branded his beloved boss a cow thief and thrown the Circle M into the clutches of Cole Garson. Most people had forgotten that Cole Garson's Bar G and Ed Yate's Flying Y had once been King Malory's Circle M ranch. Fifteen years was a long time. Even Pete Walker had almost forgotten. Pete was fine, a good man to have along in a tight place, but he was not one to hold memories of the past.

King Malory had been dead several months when Ed Yate arrived in the San Lucas country with his bunch of Texas longhorns. He had acquired a large slice of the old Circle M from Garson, and had been glad to put Sam and Pete on his new Flying Y payroll. They were familiar with the range, and Sam had soon become foreman of the outfit. Ed was a square shooter and it was his money that had helped Sam acquire the San Lucas Hotel after the stampede affair.

Puzzlement deepened in Sam's eyes as he thought about Ed Yate. Ed was one of the men who had captured young Malory and thrown him in jail. Ed was not a man who would make such serious accusations without sufficient proof. It looked bad for young Malory. And yet — *and yet —*

21

Sam's face went bleak, and he bent to a lower drawer in the desk. He fumbled for a moment, straightened up with a belt in his left hand. He buckled it on to his big waist, drew the long-barrelled forty-five from the holster, examined it carefully and pushed it back into its leather sheath. His eyes were bright now, and grim.

CHAPTER
THREE

Surprise Attack

The San Lucas jail was a long adobe building hidden in a grove of hoary cottonwood trees some quarter of a mile from the town's main street. The location, because of its distance, often drew profane comments from the succession of town marshals delegated to enforce the law, but the ancient structure offered a ready-made bastille, and the citizens of San Lucas saw no good reason to tax themselves for a new jail.

It had once been the home of a *ranchero* who had settled there a hundred or more years before General Kearney marched his troops into Santa Fe. The *ranchero* had built well, with an eye to defense from marauding Comanches and the massive mud walls had stoutly resisted the onslaught of time and weather.

A wide gallery fronted the length of the building, its mud and tule-thatched roof resting on *vigas* supported by huge, rough-axed timbers the *ranchero* had dragged down from the mountain slopes. Iron bars were now set in the small windows that overlooked the gallery, and all the doors save the main entrance had been sealed tight into the walls.

The door that led into the office was open and the dim light of a kerosene lamp silhouetted the jailer as he stood there, gazing pensively into the blanketing night, now and again taking a long pull at the whisky flask in his hand.

A voice broke the stillness, and with an angry ejaculation the jailer tilted the flask to his lips, drained it hurriedly and hurled the bottle into the brush.

The voice came again, loud, demanding. The jailer slammed the heavy door shut and crossed the office to another door that led into the corridor. A lighted lantern stood on the floor here. He picked it up, moved down the corridor that was lined on either side with narrow wooden doors, each set with iron grills about two feet square.

He halted, lifted the lantern and peered into the cell that was the source of the complaining voice. The dim light of the lantern revealed a face peering back at him.

The jailer scowled. He was a thin-featured man with mean little eyes and a ragged, drooping mustache.

He said angrily. "You doggone cow thief, shut off yore talk."

The lantern light showed a grin on Kingman Malory's face. "I don't think much of your hotel," he said. "No water, no cigarettes, and this straw you use for beds is a disgrace."

"You fellers make me sick," fumed the jailer.

"I'd say your hotel is not very popular," continued the prisoner. "I seem to be your only guest."

"Don't keep only drunks here," the jailer told him. "We send fellers like you over to the county jail in

Deming. You'll be headin' that way soon as the sheriff comes to git you."

"I must be important," grinned his prisoner. "How about a cigarette, mister?"

"You sure got plenty nerve," sneered the jailer. He placed the lantern on the hard-packed mud floor and fished a fresh pint of whisky from his hip pocket. "I ain't handin' out smokes to no lowdown rustler." He tipped the flask to his mouth.

"Good likker," he announced. He smacked his lips, returned the flask to his pocket. "Ed Yate give it to me when him an' the other fellers brung you in." He leered drunkenly. "Ed give me *two* pints. Some hombre!"

Young King Malory was watching him intently, face pressed close to the iron bars, and the glow from the lantern showed an odd and hard glint in his eyes.

The jailer drank again, fumbled the flask back into his pocket. It was the second pint within the hour and the liquor was taking hold, arousing in him a fellow feeling for his lone prisoner. He reached for the flask he had just put away.

"Have a drink, feller? Shore is good likker."

King shook his head. "Not even whisky can cheer me up tonight."

The jailer was offended. "Ain't askin' you ag'in." He tilted the flask to his lips. "Won't drink with me, huh?"

King was watching him intently, and his placating grin did not match the hard gleam in his eyes. He said, softly, "I sure crave a smoke, mister. I'll trade you my drink of whisky for that sack of Durham in your shirt pocket."

25

The jailer eyed the flask in his hand critically. "Ain't more'n a drink or two left," he grumbled. "I shore ain't wastin' 'em on a doggone cow thief. All right, feller, it's a deal." He felt in his shirt pocket, dragged out tobacco sack and papers, leaned against the cell door to push them through the bars. Steel-hard fingers clamped over his wrist.

For a brief moment the man attempted to resist the terrific twist that was wrenching his elbow. The flask dropped, splintered on the floor. Agony contorted his face.

"Leggo!" he gasped. "You're breakin' my arm." He made an attempt to reach for his gun. King slid his other hand between the bars, got a firm hold on his hair and slammed his head savagely against the steel grill.

The jailer groaned, struggled weakly to get at his jammed holster. King gave his head another crack against the bars. Blood trickled from a long gash in his scalp.

"Yuh're killin' me!" groaned the man.

"Unlock the door," King said. "Quick, or I *will* kill you."

There was no fight left in the jailer, and while King held him, relentless grasp on wrist and hair, he fumbled for his key. The lock clicked; King gave the intoxicated man a shove that sent him reeling back from the door. He crashed hard against the opposite wall of the narrow corridor, groaned, collapsed on the floor.

King plunged through the door. A brief look told him that the jailer was unconscious. He turned the limp body over, jerked the forty-five from the man's holster and straightened up. He examined it, saw it was fully loaded, bent again over the senseless man and removed cartridge-filled belt and holster. He worked swiftly, coolly, buckled the belt over his own lean waist and pushed the Colt into the holster.

The lantern was still upright on the floor, unharmed by the brief struggle. He picked it up, held the light close to the man's blood-streaked face. He smiled grimly. The jailer had taken several nasty cracks on the head, but the wounds were superficial.

King set the lantern back on the floor, quickly unfastened the leather strap that held the man's trousers. He turned him over, pulled his arms back and tied his wrists with the belt.

He rolled him over on his back again, saw a soiled bandana in his hip pocket. He snatched it, twisted it into a gag and knotted it between the man's teeth.

He stood up, grim satisfaction in the look he bent on the helpless jailer. Of a sudden he stiffened, and his head turned in a look down the corridor to the office door which the jailer had left partly open. Lamplight made a faint glow there, threw a slow-moving shadow. He knew now that the sound he had heard was the movement of stealthy feet.

Dismay touched his face. To deal further with the man lying on the floor was out of the question, nor had he time to extinguish the lantern.

King wasted no motions. He snatched the key from the lock, slipped back into the cell, closed the door and dropped on his straw bed. He lay motionless, eyes fixed on the door, the gun in his hand.

The footsteps approached up the corridor. He heard a low exclamation, and now followed a dead silence. King held his breath, kept his gaze on the door, his gun ready. He was regretting now the impulse that had disturbed the timing of certain planned events. The drunk jailer had offered an opportunity too great for him to resist.

The prolonged stillness began to get on his nerves and he was suddenly aware of a tightness in his gun hand, a too hard press of trigger finger. An annoyed grin creased his face and he lowered the gun. No time now to let excitement unsteady him.

On the other side of the door Sam Doan and Pete Walker were gazing down at the senseless jailer plainly visible in the lantern's glow. Guns were in their lowered hands and astonishment in their eyes.

It was Pete who broke the silence. "Looks like the young feller is a jump in front of us," he said. "If my eyes ain't gone plumb loco this here hawgtied gent is Kansas Jones, gardeen of the San Lucas jail."

"Sure is," Sam Doan said. "Looks like he's been drinkin' plenty. We seen him toss that flask into the scrub when we was watchin' him stand there in the door, and here's 'nother bottle layin' broke on the floor."

"Got his head broke plenty, too," commented Pete. "Somebody sure layed his skelp wide open from the looks of that blood." There was no mirth in the chuckle that came from his throat. "Saves me the job of layin' the end of my gun flat on his skull before he got a look at us, Sam."

"That's right," agreed Sam. "We sure wasn't wantin' Kansas to know who it was bustin' into his jail." He bent low, studied the blood-smeared face. "He ain't hurt much, Pete. From the way he's snortin' I'd say he's just mostly drunk and sleepin' it off."

"That crack on the haid sure makes him sleep more sound," Pete Walker said with another mirthless chuckle.

Sam picked up the lantern, turned its light on the cell door, raised it higher and peered through the iron grill. He lowered the lantern, and the dim light showed a perplexed look on his face.

"Layin' there on the straw," he whispered. "Looks like he's asleep, only it don't seem natcheral he could be sleepin'."

Pete's hand motioned at the jailer's limp body. "Kansas ain't wearin' his gun. Cartridge belt gone, too."

The two old-timers exchanged puzzled looks, and after a moment, Sam bent his head, stared at the cell door. "Ain't locked," he muttered. "Sure is queer business, Pete."

Gently, careful to make no sound, he inched the door open and stepped inside the cell, came to an abrupt standstill.

There was no mistaking what the light of the lantern in his hand revealed. The muzzle of a gun pointing directly at his middle.

Sam heard a muttered exclamation from behind him. He said softly, "Easy, Pete. He's got us covered."

King Malory was suddenly on his feet. The gun, steady in his hand, menaced them, and for a long moment the only sound there was the stertorous breathing of the senseless jailer.

It was Sam Doan who broke the silence. He said, quietly, "No call for you to hold that gun on us, young feller."

"Talk some more," King said, grim, unsmiling. "I'm in a hurry."

"I seen that business back at the store when you climbed down from the stage," Sam continued. "Heard you admit to the name of King Malory."

"That's right." King's eyes narrowed. "What about it?"

"We ain't likin' what they done to you," Sam told him. "We was with old King Malory when he made the drive across the *Jornado del Muerto*. You've got the look of him, son. We figger you're mebbe some kin."

A curious expression softened the hard gleam in the prisoner's eyes. He nodded. "I'm his grandson."

A smile spread over Sam's face. "That's how come Pete and me is here," he said simply. "We figgered to bust you out of this jail. You can't be old King's grandson and be a cow thief."

The young man studied him attentively. "You've only my word for it that I'm his grandson," he said.

"You're the spittin' image of him," Sam declared. "If you claimed different, I'd say you was a liar."

A slow grin took the hardness from King's face. "I'm not giving you that chance, old-timer." His face sobered again and he added softly, "I never saw my grandfather."

"Old King was murdered," Sam Doan said in a harsh voice. "Pete and me ain't lettin' 'em murder his grandson, not while we can lift a gun."

"Murdered!" Young King Malory's voice was a husky whisper. "You know that for a fact, mister?" He slowly pushed the gun into its holster, stood there, bitter gaze on them.

Sam shook his head. "Never could prove nothin'." His voice was a groan. "We only knowed that when they hung old King for a cow thief it was plain murder. There ain't no other answer. He was murdered."

"That's one reason that brings me to San Lucas." King spoke quietly. "I could never believe that my grandfather was a cow thief. I'm going to clear his name if I die doing it."

The two older men gazed at him, approval in their eyes.

"Has the same way of talkin', huh, Pete?" muttered Sam.

"Sure has," agreed Pete. His eyes gleamed. "You can count on us, young feller. We're ridin' with you same as we rode with old King."

"*Gracias.*" King's smile was back, warm, friendly, and there was a hint of excitement in his eyes. "Gives me a queer feeling, meeting you two old-timers who knew him."

"He saved my life down on the Pecos that time we brought the herd over the *Jornado del Muerto*."

"We was kids them days," broke in Pete. "Old King l'arned us to be growed men."

"We're backin' your play to give him his good name," growled Sam.

King Malory looked at them, and something like emotion touched his face. He said softly, his voice not quite steady, "He picked good friends when he picked you."

"We figger to be *your* friends now," Sam told him. He thrust out a big hand. "We're shakin' on it, young feller."

The three men exchanged clasps, their expressions very sober, and Sam went on, "I'm Sam Doan. Me and Pete Walker here are pardners in the San Lucas Hotel. We don't ride range no more since the stampede that stove us up some."

"Ain't so stove up but what we can lick our weight in wildcats," chuckled Pete. He grinned. "So you wasn't waitin' for nobody to bust you out of this doggone calaboose, huh. Sure one chip off the old block, son. Old King wasn't one to set 'round no time waitin' for help."

Old King Malory's grandson gave them a grim smile. "About time we're getting away from this place," he said.

They followed him into the corridor, lantern dangling from Sam's steel hook. King bent over the bound and gagged jailer who was showing signs of regaining consciousness.

"Throw him in the cell," Sam suggested.

King and Pete dragged the man inside the cell. King fished the key from his pocket, turned the lock and repocketed the key.

"Lucky for us the town marshal didn't get back from his trip to Las Cruces," chuckled Pete. "Cliff Burl is one mean hombre. He'll sure raise plenty hell when he sees what you done to Kansas."

"Kansas laid himself wide open," King said. "Too fond of his whisky."

"Drunk or sober, he's pizen mean," Sam commented. "You sure took a awful chance, son. Cain't figger yet how come you busted loose on him."

They went stealthily down the corridor to the office. Sam blew out the lantern and set it on the floor. Pete closed and locked the door behind them, slipped the key into his pocket, and gave King a contented grin.

"Looks like we're all set to get you on the jump away from here," he said.

The dim light from the lamp on the desk touched King Malory's face, showed a curious look of indecision that puzzled the two older men.

"Ain't you trustin' us?" Sam's tone was gruff.

"You wouldn't have had the chance to ask me that question if I was not trusting you," answered King. "It's like this, Sam, there's a lot you and Pete don't know about this business."

Worry deepened in Sam Doan's lined face. He spoke sorrowfully, "You ain't saying' it's true about you bein' on the dodge from the law, son?"

"It's hard to explain," King answered. "There are things I want to tell you, and right now there are reasons why I must keep my mouth shut."

"Are you admittin' you're a cow thief, son?" Sam looked stricken. He went on, not waiting for an answer. "Pete and me won't never believe it only 'less you tell us your own self."

King shook his head, and again some deep emotion fleetingly touched his face. He started to speak, reached instead for his gun and crouched low behind the desk.

Sam and Pete heard the sound now, stealthy footsteps outside. They moved swiftly, silent as Indians and pressed close to the wall behind the door.

It was not locked, and after a moment's silence the door swung slowly open. A man stepped inside, stood listening. Two more men followed him, and suddenly Sam's foot reached out and slammed the door shut.

CHAPTER
FOUR

Escape

The slam of the door, Sam's harsh voice, held the newcomers rigid. They sensed that death was breathing on their necks.

"Reach high," ordered Sam. He slid into view, gun menacing them.

They obeyed, lifted their hands. Sam's angry gaze fastened on the tallest of the trio.

He said furiously, "You ain't takin' him, Ed. I'm squeezin' trigger first move one of you coyotes makes."

Ed Yate's face was a study in astonishment. His eyes bulged. "What are you two old longhorns trying to pull off?" he asked in a choked voice.

"Same question goes for you," retorted the former Flying Y foreman. "What for you and Holcomb and Barr come sneakin' 'round here? Figger to take young Malory out and swing him private, huh?" Rage tightened his voice. "You ain't doin' it, Ed Yate. Not while Pete and me can make gunsmoke."

The three men gazed at him, speechless, exchanged sickly grins that froze on their faces when they suddenly saw King Malory smiling amusedly at them from behind the desk.

"Take it easy, Yate," he said quietly. "No harm done if we handle this right."

"What's the big idea?" The Flying Y man's face was an angry red. "Trying to pull off some kind of double cross?" His furious look went to his one-time foreman. "You old range wolf, quit pointing that damn gun at me."

Sam's forty-five remained as it was, but he risked a puzzled glance at the younger man standing by the desk. Pete kept his wary eyes hard on Yate's companions, fingers wrapped over gun butt. The deepening scowl on his face showed that he shared Sam's growing uneasiness.

"No double cross, Yate," King's smile broadened, put a hint of sun-wrinkles around his eyes. "Just a little misunderstanding. You see, these old-timers are good friends of mine, used to ride for my grandfather down on the Pecos. They didn't like you throwing me in your smelly jail."

Laughter suddenly replaced the anger in Ed Yate's eyes. He started to lower his hands, changed his mind when he met Sam's warning look. He said impatiently, "All right, Malory. Get a rope on these fighting long-horns before they start trouble."

Sam suddenly exploded. "That's right, son. Talk awful fast. I no savvy this business and I sure ain't likin' it."

King looked questioningly at Ed Yate. "We've got to tell them," he said.

Yate exchanged glances with Holcomb and Barr. They nodded, and the deputy marshal said dryly, "You can't tell 'em too quick for me, not with that little feller's gun ready to empty lead my way."

King nodded, met Sam's grim look. "I was telling you there were things you didn't understand," he said. "I wanted to explain, but I'd promised not to talk." He gestured. "These men are friends, too, but nobody in San Lucas is supposed to know they are."

Sam lowered his gun, pushed it into his holster. "No savvy." His eyes under shaggy brows were hard, angry. "I'm still not likin' it."

"They threw you in jail," blurted Pete, tight-lipped, wrathful. "How come, young feller?"

"Don't blame you for feeling the way you do," grinned King. "I didn't know I had friends like you in town, and I reckon Ed Yate didn't, or he would have told you about our plan to make everybody think I'm an outlaw. It seemed a good idea to pull off that play when I climbed from the stage."

Sam and Pete exchanged baffled looks, and Sam said grimly, "Talk some more."

King said again, "Take it easy, Sam." There was affection, admiration in his eyes, his warm smile. "It's mighty fine to run into friends like you and Pete, but it wasn't in the plan for you to come and break me out of jail."

Pete Walker slapped a lean thigh, gave Ed Yate a delighted look. "Listen to him, Ed! Talks and acts like his fightin' old granpappy. He busted hisself out of that cell before Sam and me got here. Had Kansas laid out cold on the floor, bleedin' like a stuck hawg." Pete rocked on his heels, grinned around happily. "Old King hisself never acted more smart in a tight hole."

King shrugged, gave Ed Yate a brief grin. "It was that quart of whisky you gave him that did the trick," he said. "Seemed a waste of time to wait for you and Holcomb to show up."

The Flying Y man nodded. His expression indicated he understood. "Kansas never could hold his liquor," he commented. He smiled complacently at his two companions. "Told you we'd find Kansas too drunk to know he was jailer here."

Deputy Marshal Holcomb broke his silence. "We should get away from this place. No sense pressing good luck." His voice showed taut nerves.

"No need to worry," smiled Yate. "I took care that Town Marshal Burl won't get back from Las Cruces tonight."

Sam Doan's frowning gaze was on his one-time boss. He said with some heat, "I reckon Kansas wasn't so drunk, Ed. You should see that gash on his haid. I ain't figgered it yet how come King got to the skunk." He paused, perplexed look on King. "This here business has got me stumped. What for this idee to make folks think you're a lowdown cow thief."

King gave Yate a look. "*You* tell them."

Ed Yate nodded, said laconically, "Malory is working for the San Lucas Stockmen's Association."

Sam and Pete stared at him, astonishment and relief in their eyes, and Sam said reproachfully, "Doggone you, Ed! Seems like you could be trustin' Pete and me after all the years we put in with the old Flyin' Y."

His former boss frowned. "It's a close secret, Sam. We don't want it known that Malory's game is to get on friendly terms with this bunch of cow thieves that are rustling us to the bone."

"I reckon we savvy," grunted Sam.

"Somebody with brains is running the gang," Deputy Marshal Holcomb said. "We want to track him down and it was Yate's idea to pull off this play."

"I savvy," repeated Sam. "The idee is to get the gang thinkin' he's sure one cow stealin' outlaw who's bust loose from jail and is on the dodge." He gave Pete a delighted grin. "Old King hisself, huh?"

"Chip right off the old block," chuckled Pete.

"We've gone to a lot of trouble," Holcomb continued, stern look on them. "Rigged up a story in the Santa Fe *Republican* that Malory is a notorious desperado."

"We seen that story," interrupted Pete. "Sam come near chokin' to death, he was so hawg-wild."

The U. S. deputy marshal gestured impatiently. "This business is no joke," he went on. "It's a matter of life or death for Malory. Nobody save ourselves knows that Malory is a secret investigator for the Association. A leak will surely mean his death."

Sam nodded, said soberly, "King can count on Pete and me, Holcomb. We savvy what he's goin' up ag'inst."

"We staged the play back at the store to get folks fooled," the deputy marshal continued in his thin, hard voice. "We want the news to reach the man who's bossing this bunch of cow thieves. The idea is that our unknown rustler chief will invite Malory to join his gang."

"Won't be easy," worried Sam. "Ain't likin' the idee so much. King won't last long if he goes and makes a wrong move."

"Don't you worry, old-timer," smiled King. His face hardened. "Hunting down this pack of range wolves is only *part* of my job." He spoke slowly, significantly. "You know what I mean, Sam."

Sam and Pete exchanged looks, and Sam said grimly, "I reckon we savvy, King."

"Let's finish this business," drawled Barr. "No sense wasting time here, risking discovery."

"That's right," agreed Yate. "Everything is all set for the getaway."

"Got a bronc ready for him?" Sam asked.

The Flying Y man nodded. "Cached outside in the chaparral. King forks him, heads west for the border, makes a play of hightailing it across town, yelling and shooting his gun. Bravado stuff to show the town no jail can hold *him*."

Sam shook his head, said disgustedly, "Ain't good sense."

"Sure it's good sense," argued Yate. "We want folks excited, talking about how King Malory broke jail. It's talk that will make a hit with the gang King wants to run into, get friendly with."

Sam nodded. "Mebbe you're right at that, Ed," he was forced to agree.

"You bet he's right," declared the deputy marshal. "We've planned this thing carefully, Doan."

Ed Yate went on talking. "We're giving Malory ten or fifteen minutes, then Holcomb, Barr and myself are rounding up a posse and setting out in chase." Yate's eyes twinkled. "Only we'll head *south*, which means we won't *ever* pick up Malory's trail."

Barr broke in, laughter in his voice. "Next week's *Republican* will have a piece telling how the notorious King Malory escaped from the San Lucas jail."

"I reckon it builds up," admitted Sam. He gave King a wintry smile. "Will listen good to this lowdown coyote you aim to read sign on."

King nodded, unbuckled the jailer's gunbelt. "You've got my own with the horse?" he asked Yate.

"Hanging on the saddlehorn," Ed Yate assured him.

King tossed the discarded gun and belt under the desk, smiled around at the intent face. "Let's go," he said.

Sam lifted a hand. "Listen." There was a grim resolve in his voice. "Pete and me is ridin' with you a ways."

The deputy marshal started to protest, was suddenly silent under King's hard look.

"Sam and Pete rode stirrup to stirrup with my grandfather." King spoke softly. "They were his friends, and now they are *my* friends." He paused, and harsh lines suddenly aged his face. "I'm thinking of something a man wrote when I was a kid in Boston. I'd just been told about my grandfather being hanged for a cow thief. It wasn't news I could believe. I'd never seen him, but his letters had taught me a lot, taught me about things that went into making a *man*. I knew he

41

could not have been guilty of stealing cows or doing anything unworthy of his code."

King paused again, his gaze on Pete and Sam. "You were more lucky than I was," he said in the same quiet voice. "You knew my grandfather, whose name I bear."

Sam nodded, said gruffly, "Old King l'arned Pete and me that a man don't never cheat no time. It was always fair and square with him, even when bein' fair meant his hurt. He'd say he'd ruther be right and lose than be wrong and win."

"Yes," King said, his voice husky. "He'd write that way to me." He paused, his expression thoughtful. "I told you I was thinking of something a man wrote. He said, 'Whoever fights, whoever falls, justice conquers evermore.' My grandfather fell because of injustice. I promised myself that I would carry on the fight until justice conquered — until I had won back his good name."

There was a long silence, broken by Sam Doan. "We figger to ride the justice trail with you, son. We ain't quittin' until that black shame is lifted from old King's name."

Young King Malory's eyes blazed. "Now you know the *real* reason why I've taken on this job with your Association," he said to Ed Yate. "It's my guess that the man who is the brains of this gang is the man who murdered my grandfather." He was suddenly moving swiftly to the door. "Let's go."

They trooped after him into the shadowed night, and Sam grasped his arm, said softly, "We'll be waitin' where the creek forks, couple of miles west of town."

King stood for a moment, gaze on his two new friends as they disappeared into the blanketing darkness. His boyish smile was back again.

"All right," he said to Ed Yate. "Where's this horse you got cached out here. I'm on my way."

CHAPTER
FIVE

Mesquite Springs

The shimmering heat waves hurt Mary Carroll's eyes and unable for the moment to keep her gaze on the slow-moving herd she drew her sweat-lathered horse to a standstill. She had never felt so heartsick, so keenly aware of imminent disaster. It was in her mind that she hated this vast land of bristling cacti and greasewood, the parched brown hills.

She heard her father's voice, a harsh croak that made her wince. "We've got to keep 'em moving," he said. "Only a couple of miles now to water."

Mary's head lifted in a despairing look at him. "They're dying on their feet." She spoke hopelessly. "They can't make it."

Jim Carroll gestured wearily. The beaten look of him as he drooped there in his saddle sent a stab of pity through the girl.

She offered no comment, returned her gaze to the gaunt flanked cattle down in the wash. They seemed hardly to move, heads low, swinging with each labored step. Their sullen bawls tortured her.

The wash, actually the bed of a creek made dry by the long drought, twisted up between low brown hills baked to lifelessness under the relentless sun. No living thing stirred there save the thirst-maddened cattle.

She lifted a hand against the fierce glare of the sun and gazed across the blistering reach of sand. She knew that beyond the low ridge was the water that could save this pitiful remnant of her father's herd. They must not only reach Mesquite Springs, they must be allowed to drink, slake their thirst to the full.

This last thought built a new fear in her, deepened her misgivings.

She said, worriedly, "Cole Garson won't let us water the herd at the Springs. You know how he hates you."

"He's a cowman," reminded her father. "Not even his kind of range hog will stand by and see cows die for water." His tone lacked conviction.

"Dal Santeen said Garson has put up barbed wire," Mary reminded.

Jim Carroll scowled. "I'll damn quick cut the wires."

"He'll have men posted there," Mary told him with a hopeless gesture.

Her father was silent for a long moment, then slowly his gaunt frame stiffened in his saddle, his sunburned face hardened and his hand dropped to the butt of the gun in its holster.

"Barbed wire or gunsmoke, I'm watering the cows at Mesquite Springs," he said with grim finality.

She rode with him down the slope and crossed the wash, lifted her voice in shrill yips at the bellowing herd, and despite the scorching heat of the noonday sun her heart was a cold lump in her. She knew her father's small patience against opposition, the turbulent nature of him that so easily flared to violence. Blood would be spilled if Cole Garson's men tried to turn the herd back from the water, and her father would be only one against many. The thought appalled her.

She became aware of a change in the movement of the herd, a quickening that began with the bawling steer in the lead. In an instant the long line of cattle broke into a shambling run that, but for their weakness, would have been a stampede.

"Smell water!" shouted her father. He spurred his horse into a lope. The fierce glint hot in his eyes drew a shiver from the girl. It meant water now, for the thirsting JC cattle, or dead men — her father *dead*.

She urged her own tired horse into a slow run, stifled a little cry as she saw a cow suddenly stagger and go down. It lay there, sides heaving, staring eyes glassy.

Jim Carroll pulled his horse to a quick standstill, glowered at the stricken animal. No word came from him, and after a moment his fingers closed over his gun butt.

Mary looked away, pushed on after the lumbering herd. She felt sick, but knew it was the only thing her father could do — make the end quick and merciful.

She heard the sharp crack of the forty-five, and then the thud of hoofs as her father rode to overtake her. He passed her, pushing the gun back into holster, his face bleak, forbidding.

The crazed cattle were close to the top of the hill now, the weaker animals slowing down, but stumbling blindly forward, the smell of water in their nostrils an irresistible magnet that held them true to the course.

Through the swirling dust Mary glimpsed a horseman skylined on the ridge. For a brief moment the lone rider held his horse motionless, then suddenly he was gone.

Mary's heart turned over. The crisis was upon them. She swung her mare, rode quickly to her father's side, a frantic impulse in her to shield him. Not even Cole Garson's hard-bitten men would be ruthless enough to shoot at the risk of harming a girl.

Jim Carroll had not seen the horseman. He was too busy prodding the laggards up the hill. He gave the girl an elated grin, brushed dust from bloodshot eyes.

"Told you we'd get 'em to water," he exulted.

Mary hardly heard his words. She was striving desperately to think of some way to avert the coming clash, and now her look fastened on the gun in his holster. She must get the forty-five away from him. To find himself balked at the last moment would drive Jim Carroll into a frenzy. She knew with sickening certainty that he would use that gun if Cole Garson's riders tried to keep the herd from the springs.

Another cow was suddenly down, and in an instant Mary leaned close to her father and snatched the Colt from his belt.

"You keep going!" she shouted. "I — I'll do it."

Jim Carroll nodded, pushed up the slope, vanished in yellow swirls of dust. Mary reined over to the fallen cow. Her heart was thumping madly. Her ruse had worked, giving her possession of the gun.

She hesitated, nerving herself to squeeze the trigger, and end the sufferings of the stricken animal. Her courage failed her. It was too much like murder.

She bent low from her saddle for a closer look, saw with a wave of relief that the cow was already dead. No need to use the gun. She whirled the mare away, halted again. Her father would wonder if he failed to hear the expected gunshot. He might not believe that the cow was dead and would return to finish the job himself.

She came to a swift decision. She must not give him a chance to ask for the gun. He was in less danger without it. The Bar G riders would not shoot an unarmed man — not unless they were cold-blooded murderers.

Deliberately she fired a shot into the air and, smoking gun in hand, sent the mare into a fast run up the slope. Her father yelled at her as she tore past him. She pretended not to hear. He was not going to have his fortyfive back — not until this business was finished.

Some score of the steers were topping the ridge, and mad now for the water so close to them they went scampering down the slope, tails up.

Mary kept the mare at a fast lope, headed straight for the group of men beyond the barbed-wire fence. She heard a voice, thin, malevolent:

"Turn those cows back, ma'am!"

She was less than five yards from the fence now, heard the crash and hum of the barbed wires as the first bunch of cattle piled against it. It was a strong fence and withstood the shock, and the steers, bawling

48

disconsolately, began a lumbering run along the barricade that kept them from the big pool of water. Two of them lay dead, necks broken by the impact. Others were limping.

Mary reined to a standstill, the gun dangling in her hand. She looked at it, suddenly tossed it over the fence.

"He's unarmed," she spoke breathlessly. "Don't hurt him."

The men looked at her, grim, silent. The entire herd was over the ridge now, streaming down the slope. A quick look told her that her father was coming.

She spoke again, desperately, pleadingly, addressing the man who had warned her to turn the herd back.

"Please, Mr. Garson, the cattle are dying! You *must* let them get to the water!"

Cole Garson glowered at her from his saddle. He was a skinny little man with a tight-lipped mouth under a great beak of a nose. A large black hat shadowed watchful, naked-lidded eyes set under hairless brows. He wore a black silk shirt and black trousers tucked into black boots. He looked like a vulture perched there on the tall black horse.

He broke his silence. "Jim Carroll is not watering his cows here," he said.

Mary's look went to the three riders slouching at ease in their saddles. Their expressionless faces told her nothing. She recognized one of them, Sandy Wells. She had danced with him at the roundup ball held once a year in San Lucas. She had rather liked him, and at this moment she thought she saw a hint of pity in his

49

startling blue eyes. Whatever his emotions, he made no effort to help her. She did not blame him. The word of his boss was the law that governed him.

She realized that none of these men could have been the lone rider she had glimpsed on the ridge. The thought grew in her that they were not aware of the stranger's presence up in the piñon scrub.

More cattle were piling against the fence. Jim Carroll's angry voice lifted above the clamor.

"Somebody get that gate open!" he yelled. "I'm watering my cows here and nobody is going to stop me!" He pulled his winded horse to a standstill, furious gaze on Cole Garson. "You damn skunk!" he frothed. "You figger you've got me by the short hair, huh? Figger to ruin me!"

The little man on the tall black horse rubbed his chin with a clawlike hand. "I'll make a deal," he said in his thin voice. "Some three hundred head here. Give me my pick of half of 'em and you can have your water."

"Deal nothin'!" shouted Carroll. "Get that gate open or I'll start trouble right now!" His hand fumbled at the empty holster and now he gave his daughter a startled look. "My gun!" he yelled. "I want my gun, Mary!"

His gaze followed her gesture, fastened on the long-barrelled Colt lying in the dust on the far side of the fence. He muttered a shocked ejaculation, swung his head in an incredulous look at Mary.

She said, stiff-lipped, "It's better there than in your hand."

She dared a furtive glance up the slope, and something she glimpsed sent a tingle through her. A shape that moved in the scrub, became motionless at the turn of her head.

It was Cole Garson who broke the brief silence. "The girl's right." His voice came sharp above the bedlam of the crazed cattle. "Don't want bloodshed, Jim Carroll. Get your cows away from here."

Jim Carroll leaned heavily on his saddle horn. There was a gray, beaten look to him. His lips moved convulsively as if trying to form words.

Mary spoke for him, her voice edged with bitterness. "You can't do this cruel thing, Mr. Garson."

He gazed back at her, eyes cold, unwinking, devoid of emotion.

"I'm doin' it," he answered.

"They'll die," she cried fiercely.

"Not *my* cows," Cole Garson said.

Mary's look covered the riders. Their grim faces told her she could expect no help from them.

"You're not cowmen!" she flared. "You're a pack of cowards, all of you!" Angry tears smarted in her eyes. "I wish I'd kept the gun! I'd have used it."

A chortle came from one of the riders. "Wildcat, huh," he said. He rolled suddenly amused eyes at the others. "Reckon it's mighty lucky for us she *did* throw her dad's smokepot over the fence."

Jim Carroll came out of his daze, glared angrily at the speaker. "That's enough from you, feller." His look went briefly to the crazed cattle bellowing around the barricade, returned to Cole Garson, silent, watchful, hunched like a buzzard on his black horse.

"I'm cutting the wires, Garson," he said. "Mesquite Springs don't belong to you. I've a right to the water."

"It's *my* fence," replied the owner of Bar G. "No man cuts those wires without my say-so."

"To hell with your say-so!" exploded Carroll. He swung from his saddle. "I'm cutting those wires."

"No!" Garson said, and as if the word was a signal, his Bar G riders were instantly reaching for their guns.

Mary stifled a cry, jumped her mare between Carroll and the fence.

"It's no use!" she said frantically. "They'll kill you!"

Jim Carroll was breathing hard. He stood motionless, hand clutching the wire-cutters at his belt, safe for the moment from the threatening guns. He said in a choked voice, "Don't interfere. I'm cutting the wires."

"Don't move!" implored Mary. "They only want an excuse to start shooting."

"The girl's right again," Cole Garson said with a dry cackle. "It's *my* fence. I'm within the law. Be your own fault if you get shot tryin' to cut it."

"You want to ruin me," accused Jim Carroll furiously.

"I aim to run you out of the country," admitted the owner of Bar G. "Ain't likin' cow thieves neighborin' my range."

Jim Carroll was suddenly rigid, and when he spoke his voice was a harsh whisper. "I'll kill you for that lie, Cole Garson. I'll kill you for saying I'm a cow thief."

The threat left Garson unperturbed. "You won't get the chance, Carroll. You've asked for a showdown, and you'll have it with a rope round your neck and the nearest tree that's handy."

"No!" cried Mary. "You monster! Don't you dare lay a hand on my father!"

A stillness settled over the scene, broken only by the despairing bawls of the cattle moving slowly around the barricade seeking an entrance to the big pool under the mesquite trees.

A voice came from somewhere on the hillside above the fence, and the sound of it sheared through that silence like cold steel.

"You buzzard on the black horse, I've got you covered. Tell your killers to drop their guns."

Cole Garson was suddenly rigid, a man turned to stone, his face a gray mask under the shadowing black hat. One of the riders muttered a curse. Garson's eyes blasted him.

"I'm not waiting," warned the voice.

Garson spoke, his voice a croak. "Drop your guns, boys."

The Bar G riders swung their heads, looked at him, and again he whispered the command.

Rage and resentment stark in their hard faces, they sullenly obeyed, lifted hands high in response to another curt command from the hillside.

Jim Carroll was already wriggling under the barbed wires. He swooped for the guns, straightened up, a forty-five in each hand, his grim gaze on the disarmed men.

"Good work!" applauded his unseen deliverer. "I'll be right down and join the party."

Mary's father grinned at his prisoners. "Climb down from your broncs," he ordered. "Step back from 'em and keep your hands reachin' high."

They obeyed, sullen angry men; stood there, backs to him, hands above their heads. Mary rode close to the fence and Carroll handed her the third gun. She leveled it at Cole Garson.

Her coolness at that moment astonished her. Death had reached so perilously near to her father. And for herself had threatened a like fate, or worse. Cole Garson would not have wanted her around to tell the tale of his infamy. He would have made a clean finish of the business.

The swift turn of events had not entirely surprised her. She knew now that she had been keyed up for something to happen. Ever since she had realized that the lone rider was not one of Garson's outfit she had been aware of a strange, wild hope. She knew that never again would she hear music so sweet as the sound of that voice from the hillside. She half expected to see an angel appear with great white wings and a flaming sword.

CHAPTER
SIX

Mary Makes a Promise

The footsteps that she heard were human enough, the quick rap of high bootheels. The man's glance as he passed exploded a shock in her. Surprised recognition held her rigid. He was the same man she had seen arrested as he climbed from the stage in front of the store. He had made a daring escape later that night, ridden like a yelling Comànche down the street, past the livery barn where she was waiting for her father to harness the buckboard team for the long, midnight drive back to the ranch.

He had seen her standing there under the glare of the big swing lantern, waved a gay salute as he tore past. An outlaw, a border desperado, a fugitive from the law; and now he was here, gun menacing Cole Garson.

He was under the fence now, and confronting Garson.

"Climb down," he ordered.

Garson obeyed, tight-lipped, silent. No hint of recognition touched his stony face.

King felt him over with expert hands. "No gun on you."

"I never carry a gun," Garson told him.

"Hire your killings done, huh?" King's tone was edged with contempt.

"You're heading for a lot of trouble, young man. I'm Cole Garson."

King gave him a mirthless smile. "The pleasure is all yours, mister. Right now I want those two gates opened in a hurry. They're chain locked. I want the key that unlocks 'em."

"Don't need a key," called Jim Carroll. He waggled one of his guns. "Got a key here that'll open *those* locks."

King nodded. "Hop to it. Your cows are mighty eager to get belly-deep in that pond."

"Should tie up these fellers, first," worried Carroll.

"I'll watch 'em." King gestured. "Prod 'em under the fence."

The three Bar G men, followed by Garson, crawled under the wires, stood in a cluster, hands above their heads. Mary Carroll studied the sullen faces. No sign there of recognition. It was apparent that none of these men had been in San Lucas the previous night, or they would have known about King Malory.

It was equally plain to her that her father also was unaware of their young rescuer's identity. Jim Carroll was too furiously preoccupied for more than a casual glance at the man who had so miraculously appeared in the nick of time. His one thought now was to get the frantic herd to the pond.

He went on the run to the nearest gate, bent over the heavy chain, and in another moment a bullet from his forty-five had smashed the lock. He began dragging the long gate open.

"All right, Mary!" he yelled.

She was already circling the milling cattle, turning them toward the opening. Her father watched, contentment on his weathered face as the herd streamed through in a mad stampede for the pond under the mesquites.

Cole Garson broke his silence. "What are you going to do next, when you finish playing the fool here?" There was contempt in his thin smile. "You can't hope to make this stick, young man."

"Well," drawled King, "it's going to stick long enough for those cows to have a good wallow in that pond."

Garson thought it over for a moment, nodded, said resignedly, "All right, you win this time. Jim Carroll can use the springs for a few days. All I want is to get away from here. Let us have our horses and we'll leave you to it and make no more trouble."

King shook his head. "You're leaving here on foot," he said. "In fact, Mr. Garson, you and your hired killers are taking a long walk. How long depends on how far it is to your home ranch."

Garson lost his icy calm. Rage and horror convulsed his face. "It's all of fifteen miles," he spluttered. "You can't do this to me!"

"You'll know different by the time you get back to your ranch," King drawled. He gave Jim Carroll a satisfied grin as the rancher came up, glanced briefly at

Mary, busy turning the stragglers toward the opened gate.

"You're shorthanded," he commented.

Jim Carroll shrugged. "Two years of drought cleaned out the payroll money." Renewed hope gleamed in his reddened eyes. "I can pull through if I can save the cows, get some fat back on the steers in time for fall market." He flung Cole Garson a fierce look. "Seems like Garson figgered to put me out of business."

The Bar G man craned his head, looked at him. "Don't crow too loud, Carroll. You ain't heard the last of this business."

Jim Carroll's hands tightened over the butts of the guns he held. "I should fix you here and now," he muttered.

King said curtly, "No gunplay!"

Something familiar in the quiet, chill voice, drew a suddenly attentive look from Carroll. His jaw sagged and startled recognition widened his eyes.

Mary came up on her sweat-lathered mare, correctly interpreted her father's astonishment. She gave him a warning look, spoke hurriedly to divert attention from him. It was her impression that Cole Garson was too interested in the amazement plain on Jim Carroll's face.

"Five of them are down, Dad," she said. Her hand lifted in an unhappy gesture.

He understood what she meant he must do, understood too that he must say nothing that might betray the identity of the man who had befriended them in their hour of great peril. He nodded, strode up the fence toward the prostrate cattle.

Mary's look fastened on Cole Garson, her face pale as she tried to ignore the five quick shots. She said fiercely, "It's your fault! You should pay us for them!"

Cole Garson was doing some fast thinking. He said in his thin, precise voice, "I don't like the idea of a fifteen mile walk back to the ranch. Not in this heat. If you can persuade your friend to let us have our horses, I'll pay cash for those dead steers."

King met the girl's questioning look. He shook his head. "No deal, Garson," he drawled. "Those broncs are four good aces right now, and we're holding on to 'em."

One of the Bar G men said bitterly, "Let's git started on the damn walk. I sure crave to git my hands down."

Jim Carroll came up, reloading his emptied gun. Garson appealed to him, repeated the offer. The JC man's haggard face brightened. "I could use the money," he muttered. "How much you figger to pay me, Garson?"

"Market price." Something like triumph put a momentary gleam in Garson's eyes.

Carroll hesitated. "It's got to be cash," he said. "Cash in my hand right now."

Garson shook his head impatiently. "Don't carry so much money loose with me." He paused, added quickly, "Best I can do is to give you a note to Vince Lestang. Vince will give you the cash. He owes me for a bunch of steers he aims to run on his new Calabasas range."

King interrupted the conversation, his voice curt. "No trade," he said.

Jim Carroll lifted his head in a resentful look at him. King gave him no chance to speak. "We're keeping the horses here." He spoke firmly. "Don't let Garson fool you, Carroll, or do you want the whole Bar G outfit on your neck before sundown?"

An angry red stained the JC man's face as he now realized the motive that had prompted Garson's offer. "I reckon that's right." He glared at Garson. "You crawlin' snake!"

King caught Mary's eye. He gestured up the slope. "Left my horse up there behind that split boulder."

She understood, nodded, pushed up the slope. They waited in silence until she returned with a rangy buckskin horse on a lead rope. King took the rope from her and swung up to the saddle.

Jim Carroll asked worriedly, "How long should I hold these broncs? Don't want Garson to rig up a charge of horse stealin' against me."

"I'd say turn 'em lose about sundown." King grinned at the sullen faces. "Not much chance our friends can make the ranch before midnight."

"We'll be headin' right back," exploded Garson. "We'll shoot every damn cow we find here, Jim Carroll. Be too bad if we find you here."

Mary gestured helplessly. "We can't move the herd so soon," she protested.

"Plenty of good grass back of the pond," King suggested.

"I'm holdin' that grass for winter feed," Garson said angrily. "I'll hunt down every JC cow I find trespassing and skin its hide."

King paid him no attention. "Use your wire cutters," he said to Carroll. "Open up the place and let your cattle graze where they will."

"Nothin' else I can do with 'em," Carroll agreed. His face hardened in lines of grim resolve. "All right, mister. Get these wolves movin' away from here."

One of the Bar G men smothered an oath. "Sure is hell," he groaned. "Ain't never hoofed it on foot more'n a mile no time in my life."

Jim Carroll eyed him sourly. "Your broncs will maybe catch up with you by the time you hit the home corral."

The man gave him an ugly look. "I'll fix you good next time I run into you, mister," he promised. "Set you loose in the *cholla* in your bare feet."

King studied him, his expression grim. "We'll give you a dose of your own medicine," he drawled. "Pull your boots off. You're taking that walk in your socks."

The man turned pale under his sunburn. "I was only jokin'," he said.

"Get your boots off." King lifted his gun. "I am *not* joking."

The cowboy gave his companions a frantic look, saw he could expect no help from them. They were not going to risk sharing his fate. He sullenly obeyed.

"I'll be tore to ribbons," he groaned.

Cole Garson broke his silence. "We'll need water," he said. "Or is it your idea for us to die of thirst?"

61

Jim Carroll got their canteens and the four men plodded away, the bootless one cursing the sharp stones and the hot sand.

King watched them, turned his head in a look at Carroll. "You'll head back for your ranch?" he asked.

The JC man nodded. "Come sundown," he replied. "I'm cuttin' those wires first, so the cattle can spread out. Be sundown by the time I get done."

"Get away from here as quickly as you can," advised King.

Carroll shrugged. For the moment he was content. His cattle were belly deep in water, and back of the springs was a vast stretch of grass-covered range.

"You're leaving us?" He asked the question softly, remembering now that this young man was a fugitive outlaw, a cow thief. Like all honest cowmen he had only contempt for a rustler, was a firm believer in the rough and ready law of gun and rope on the breed.

King Malory sensed the older man's troubled thoughts. "You're worried about me, Mr. Carroll," he said. "You're thinking I should be back in that jail cell."

"Never had no use for a cow thief," Carroll admitted. He shook his head. "You've put me in a fix, young feller. I'd likely be layin' here dead if you hadn't horned into the play."

"I'll be on my way," King said. He kept his look from Mary. "You owe me nothing, Mr. Carroll."

"I joined up with the new Stockmen's Association," Carroll told him. "If it wasn't that I'm owin' you my life I wouldn't let you ride away without some argument. The Association figgers to make rustlin' mighty unhealthy in the San Lucas country." He turned, gave King his back. "Get moving, young feller. I don't want to know which way you ride when the posse comes along askin' questions."

"Father!" Mary's face was crimson. "I — I'm ashamed —"

King shook his head at her. "It's all right," he reassured. He gave her a gay little smile. "*Adios, señorita*." He swung the buckskin horse away.

Mary sat very still on her mare, gaze following him. "You were mean to him," she told her father. "He risked his life to help us."

"I hate lowdown cow thieves," grumbled Carroll.

"He's no cow thief!" she stormed.

"Ed Yate ain't one to throw a man in jail without good reason," asserted Carroll. "I'm grateful for what he did, and I let him ride off. You shouldn't be askin' me to do more, daughter. If I'd done my duty as a member of the Association, I'd have put my gun on him and held him for the sheriff."

Mary looked at him. He was a tired old man, she realized with a sudden rush of pity, too completely weary in mind and body to think straight. It was up to her. She whirled the mare, tore away at a gallop.

King heard her coming, reined to a standstill, and there was a hint of impatience in him, as if he guessed her purpose.

Her color rose, but she met his look squarely. "I — I must thank you for all you have done." Her low voice faltered. "Father is just about crazy with all this worry about his cattle. He — he hardly knows, realizes what has happened and that you have saved his life."

His smile came, warm, friendly. "We couldn't let those cows die there, and all that water on the other side of the fence. Glad I happened along."

Mary looked at him steadily. "You didn't just happen along," she said. "I saw you up on the ridge. You were watching for us."

He grinned, said nothing.

"You are very mysterious," puzzled Mary. "How did you learn we were bringing the herd to Mesquite Springs?"

"You shouldn't be talking to an outlaw," he countered. "Your father won't like it."

She sensed he was laughing at her, shook her head. "You're not an outlaw," she told him flatly. "I don't understand what it is all about, but nothing can make me believe that you are a cow thief."

The bantering smile left his face. He looked at her intently. "I'm remembering that," he said softly. "I'll not forget, ever, Miss Carroll." He paused, and she had the odd feeling that his mind was racing, planning, making sure of events to follow. "Persuade your father to get off to your ranch as soon as possible. Don't be here when Garson's outfit comes back."

Her face clouded. "He won't let us use his range. He'll kill every cow he finds, and we can't move them now."

"You've done all you can about it," King said. "No use you and your father staying after sundown."

"We'll be ruined," Mary told him wearily.

King shook his head. "You go back to the ranch and forget it," he advised. "The string is not played out yet."

She stared at him, puzzled. "I don't understand."

"You don't need to understand." A hint of a smile touched his lips. "In fact you'll likely change your mind about me and wish I was still in that jail cell."

"You're trying to frighten me," she worried.

"No," King said, "I only want you to keep on trusting me, even if it comes hard."

"You are too dreadfully mysterious," complained Mary. And after a pause, "Perhaps I'm crazy, but I *do* trust you."

King gave her an enigmatic smile. "Keep it up." His hand lifted in a parting salute and the buckskin horse reared, pawed the air, surged swiftly away.

Mary watched until a low ridge hid horse and rider. She guessed that he was following the Bar G men to make sure they did not make a surprise return.

She became aware that her heart was pounding, was suddenly angry at herself. She was indeed crazy. For all she knew King Malory really was an outlaw — a cattle rustler.

She rode slowly back to the springs, her thoughts chaotic. She must say nothing to her father about the promise to keep on trusting King Malory, no matter how hard. She must begin immediately, hold onto that promise, refuse to allow doubts to creep in.

CHAPTER
SEVEN

His Own Country

King held the buckskin horse to a slow walk. It was not his purpose to overtake the four men who wearily climbed the sun-baked ridge. He found himself inclined to pity Cole Garson. The others were young, tough and hardy men, but Garson was well into his sixties and this walk could easily be too much for his strength.

The thought disturbed King. He had no liking for Cole Garson. The man was completely ruthless, a cold-blooded, merciless schemer, as proved by his treatment of Jim Carroll. Also, according to dark hints thrown out by Sam Doan, he was probably deeply involved in the tragedy that had taken the life and good name of King's grandfather.

King drew the horse off the trail and pulled to a standstill in the shade of a butte. He wanted to do some thinking, and there was a big clump of greasewood to screen him from view when the Bar G men finally gained the top of the steep slope.

He slid from the saddle, found a seat on a shaded boulder and thoughtfully made and lit a cigarette. The horse gave him an inquiring look, switched his tail at a fly and began nosing at the scant browse.

Vague doubts, conjectures, premonitions, filtered through King's mind as he sat there. Perhaps he had been a fool, taking on this job with the San Lucas Stockmen's Association. He was a cowman, not a professional range detective, and only one reason had induced him to accept Ed Yate's offer. The job meant an ideal opportunity to uncover the true facts of the mystery that had branded his grandfather a cow thief. As a secret investigator, his identity concealed under the mask of a desperate outlaw, he might possibly unravel the web of sinister intrigue that had resulted in the disgraceful death and ruin of the grandfather he had never seen.

His own father had been killed in a cavalry skirmish during the last months of the Civil War, and King, hardly more than a baby, and motherless, had been put in the care of a maternal aunt. He had been twelve when word came of his grandfather's death, and sixteen when he had left Boston and made his way to Texas. The following years had seasoned him, made a cowman of him, given him a reputation the length and breadth of the Panhandle. Cattle rustlers had learned to leave Double S Bar cows alone. It was this reputation that had attracted the attention of the newly organized San Lucas Stockmen's Association.

He had been reluctant to give up his job as foreman of the Double S Bar, but memories of his grandfather were still alive in him, kept steel hard the resolve to one day clear his name. It was in the San Lucas country in

67

southwestern New Mexico that his grandfather had settled with his herd of Texas longhorns and founded his vast Circle M ranch. The pull was too strong to resist, and within a week he was in Santa Fe and having his first talk with Ed Yate.

King dropped the stub of his cigarette, ground its red spark under boot-heel. He was aware of a vague annoyance as he thought of Ed Yate. He had said nothing at the time to the Flying Y man of his real reason for taking on the job. The surprise encounter with Sam Doan and Pete Walker, the discovery that they had once been members of his grandfather's Circle M outfit had rather forced the disclosure. It might prove unfortunate if it leaked out that he was the grandson of the late owner of the now non-existent Circle M ranch.

He pondered the matter for a few moments, decided that it was not likely Ed Yate would make a slip that might prove fatal to their plans. Nor would J. O. Barr or the U. S. deputy marshal. It was vitally necessary to build up the story that he was an outlaw. A slip of the tongue would mean disaster for the scheme to make contact with the mysterious leader of the rustlers.

Almost against his will he found himself thinking of Mary Carroll. She was in his thoughts too much, had been even since he had met her startled, pitying look the previous night when standing under the deputy marshal's menacing gun. He had glimpsed her again that same night when he raced out of San Lucas.

68

King grinned as he recalled her words at Mesquite Springs. *You didn't just happen along, you were watching for us.* She was more right than she knew. Only it was not possible for him to explain, tell her that it was Sam and Pete she must thank for his surprise appearance at Mesquite Springs.

As arranged, he had met the pair of old-timers at the fork of the creek two miles or more west of San Lucas, and they had taken him to a little log cabin in the hills.

"You can always figger to find one of us at this here shack," Sam Doan told him. "We aim to stick close as a couple of wood ticks, son. You've taken on a mansize job and no tellin' when hell's a-goin' to bust loose."

The cabin was well stocked with canned goods, flour, coffee, a side of bacon. Pete Walker went to work, and slices of bacon were soon sizzling on a pan and a pot of coffee bubbling on the stove. The pleasant odors made King realize that he was ravenous.

They told him they were joint owners of the cabin and the surrounding section of land in this wild and remote hill country. Someday they planned to make it their home, but for the present they used the place for occasional hunting trips after deer and bear and wild turkey. There was always water in the creek and plenty of firewood for the chopping.

"Ain't half a dozen folks know about Bear Creek Canyon," Sam informed King. "This here shack makes a good hideout and there'll be times she'll come in mighty handy."

King was grateful to these two old-time friends of his grandfather. They gave him much information and it was from them that he heard about Jim Carroll.

"He figgers to trail his herd over to Mesquite Springs," Sam said. "Jim's awful stubborn, hangin' on to his cows, and his JC range dry as last year's bones. He should have sold when he had the chance." Sam shook his head. "Ed Yate made him an offer, but Jim wouldn't listen to him."

"Cole Garson claims to own Mesquite Springs," Pete Walker commented. "Garson is meaner than a pizen snake. Jim won't have a chance." His tone was gloomy. "Sure am sorry for Mary. She's one grand gal."

"They was in town last night," Sam continued. "Stopped at the hotel." He paused, his expression worried. "Didn't have no chance to see 'em ag'in or I'd have done my best to talk him into sellin' his cows to Ed Yate. Like Pete says, Cole Garson won't let him water at the springs. Jim said he was headin' back to his ranch come midnight, soon as Mary had a few hours sleep. I reckon he'll have the herd movin' before sunup."

King's interest was mounting. He guessed that Mary was the girl of the buckboard.

"I saw a girl in the livery yard when I rode down the street," he said.

Sam nodded. "That would be Mary." He paused, gave King a grim smile. "She seen that play when they grabbed you off the stage. Was some sorry for you, from the way she talked."

There was a long silence. King went to the stove, filled his tin cup from the coffeepot and returned to the table.

"How far from here is this place, Mesquite Springs?" he asked abruptly.

"Ain't so fur," Sam told him. He gave Pete a glimmer of a satisfied grin. "Mebbe ten miles if a feller knows the shortcuts."

"I'm listening," King said.

"You figger to ride over that way?" Pete asked, softly.

"Soon as I grab off an hour's sleep." King's face hardened. "I don't like the idea of cows dying for water because of a neighbor's meanness."

"There'll likely be gunplay," Sam Doan warned.

King grinned. "You're not fooling me," he chuckled. "You were hoping I'd go."

The two old-timers exchanged sheepish looks, and Sam said mildly, "I reckon you're right, son, and we figger to ride along with you."

King shook his head. "I won't need you," he demurred. "If you and Pete are along, there *will* be gunplay and somebody killed."

Pete began an indignant retort. King's look silenced him. "This business calls for strategy," he said. "We don't want to make a shooting fight of it."

Sam said softly, "You talk like your grandpa, son. I reckon you got his brains." He gave the glowering Pete a contented look. "We ain't buckin' him, Pete."

King's eyes narrowed thoughtfully. He was aware of a vague uneasiness. His decision to help Jim Carroll get his cows to water had resulted in only a temporary victory. The business was not yet finished. Mary Carroll was due for another and less welcome surprise. He had given her a hint, asked her to keep on trusting him, no matter how hard. He wondered gloomily if he had asked too much of her; wondered, too, at himself for mixing into the business.

He frowned, shook his head. No sense in shutting his eyes to the fact that Mary Carroll was now the most important thing in his life. Something had happened to him. He had felt drawn to her the moment he had seen her sitting in the buckboard. He could find no word yet to explain the mystery. He only knew that she was the first girl who seemed so completely desirable. She was the motive that had drawn him to Mesquite Springs. Sam and Pete little dreamed how strong had been the pull.

He sat there on the boulder, mused for the length of another cigarette, then tied the buckskin to a stump of greasewood, took a small telescope from its leather saddle pocket, and went scrambling up the steep ascent of the butte. It was in his mind to have a look at the surrounding country from the summit.

It was a hard climb, put sweat on his face and took his breath. He began to regret the impulse to get this bird's-eye view, but changed his mind when he finally reached the top.

He crawled into the shade of a great overhang of rock, reached for the telescope and carefully studied the four men now nearing the summit of the ridge. It was a powerful glass, and he had no trouble picking out Cole Garson.

It was plain that the owner of Bar G was in trouble. He hardly seemed to move. Two of his companions were helping him. King was aware again of disturbing doubts. It was absurd to feel pity for the man. Nevertheless, worry grew in him and he began to wonder if he had perhaps sentenced Cole Garson to death.

He shrugged the thought off, impatient at himself, and for the next few minutes was absorbed in the vast sweep of the landscape. Emotions stirred in him. This had been his grandfather's country. *His own country, now.*

His face took on a grim, speculative look as he sat there, pieced the bits of information garnered from Sam and Pete. He would have to assemble these pieces, fit them into their proper places. Once the picture was complete he would find the answer to the riddle, solve the dark mystery of his grandfather's murder and the wrecking of his Circle M ranch.

The finger of suspicion pointed straight at Cole Garson, one-time lawyer. It was Garson who had promptly laid claim to Circle M, produced papers proving that he was old King Malory's partner. Oddly enough, he had later sold a huge slice of the range, together with the home ranch, to Ed Yate, a newcomer then in the San Lucas country. The southern half of the range, extending to the border, he had retained for himself, established the prosperous cattle ranch now known as the Bar G. Recently he had sold off another piece in the long valley of the Calabasas to Vince Lestang.

King's heart sank as he pondered the many baffling angles. It was not going to be easy to dig up the long-buried facts. Cole Garson was a likely suspect. He had certainly been the gainer by the tragic affair that had robbed old King Malory of life and reputation. Proving anything against Garson was a different matter. Even Sam Doan had gloomily admitted there was no definite evidence against the man. It was entirely possible that Garson and old Malory were partners, although it seemed odd that such an association should have been kept secret. It was one of the angles that had aroused Sam Doan's suspicions. He knew that his idolized boss had only contempt for the shady little lawyer. With Malory dead, no one could prove that Garson's partnership claim was fraudulent, or in any way question his documentary evidence.

King's face hardened. There was no doubt in *his* mind about the matter. Cole Garson was a crafty and clever man. It was more than possible that he had schemed to gain possession of the vast Circle M, contrived the ruthless plot that had resulted in old King Malory's shameful death.

Another angle of the affair intrigued King's thoughts. The odd fact that Ed Yate's Flying Y had once been part of the Circle M ranch. Ed Yate had not appeared in San Lucas until months after the tragedy. Sam and Pete could vouch for that. Ed had taken them into his new Flying Y outfit. They liked and trusted the tall, capable cowman. Also Ed Yate was the founder and head of the newly organized San Lucas Stockmen's Association. It was Ed who had begged him to take on the job of cleaning out the gang of rustlers and unmasking their leader. For that matter, Cole Garson was also a member of the Stockmen's Association.

The thought gave King a jolt. Cole Garson was exactly the wily type of man who could so successfully cloak his rustler activities under the mask of a respected and prosperous cowman. He had the brains, and it was apparent that his greed knew no limit.

The thing was possible, would explain Ed Yate's anxiety to keep King's identity a secret. There was a chance that Ed Yate was suspicious of Garson, but lacked proof. It was in his mind that by posing as a fellow-rustler, King would make friends with the Bar G man and unmask him.

A rueful grin touched King's lips. His first encounter with Garson was not likely to earn his friendship. He would have to do something about it. All the more reason to make final the decision that had been in his mind.

He was in haste, now, and soon was in the saddle again; riding up the slope, hat pulled low against the blinding glare of the sun now a steely shimmer above the mountains.

On the summit of the ridge he halted for a look down the slope. Only two men now, moving wearily across the chaparral.

King rode on, eyes alert, searching for Garson and the remaining Bar G man. He might have passed them, but for the buckskin's suddenly active ears. He drew rein again, saw a man's hat push above one of the boulders, met the wary look of sullen eyes.

"If I'd my gun I'd shore fill you with hot lead," the owner of the eyes said in a tired voice. "You're a low-down skunk, mister, settin' the boss afoot like you done."

King said nothing, rode around the boulder, saw Cole Garson flat on his back in the lengthening shade there. Garson's eyes glared up at him from a white, drawn face. The hate in that look sent a cold prickle through King.

He said, his voice quiet, gentle, "I made a mistake, Mr. Garson. It's plain you can't make it back to your ranch house on foot."

Something like astonishment passed over the cattleman's face. "That's right, young man," he spoke in a husky whisper, "a very big mistake."

King's eyes were suddenly on the cowboy who was on his feet now, a rock in clenched hand. He said sternly, "No nonsense from you." His hand hovered over gun butt. "Or do you want to stay here for buzzard's meat?"

The man hesitated, fingers still clenched over the rock. He was young, with sandy hair and eyes a startling blue in his tanned face. King felt a sympathy for him, almost a liking. There was good stuff in the youth, and courage and loyalty.

"You're holdin' the ace cards, I reckon," the man said. His fingers unclenched, let the rock drop to the ground.

"That's fine," King said. "Now we can talk." He was looking again at Garson in whose eyes there was a hint of wonder. "I was saying that I made a mistake," he continued. "Only thing I can do about it is to ride you back to your ranch house."

The cowboy muttered a startled ejaculation. "Fixin' to leave the boss layin' dead someplace, huh!" His voice was brittle, accusing.

Cole Garson said weakly, "I'll do the talking, Sandy." He sat up, leaned against the boulder, and there was a gleam in his eyes as he stared at King. "You mean that, young man?"

"I'll drop you off within a couple of miles of your place," King answered. He gave the older man a thin smile. "I'll want your promise not to send your outfit chasing after me."

"It's a deal," agreed Garson. "I'll promise anything to get back to the ranch alive." He grimaced. "I don't wish to become buzzard's meat, as you just called it."

"Ain't carin' for the notion," grumbled Sandy, his blue eyes full of distrust as he looked at King.

"Keep your mouth shut!" rasped Garson angrily. "If he'll ride me home on his horse, it's all right with me."

King felt no rancor toward the cowboy for his doubts. He warmed to him for his outspoken loyalty.

"He'll be safe enough, Sandy," he promised. "You can't think of anything better, can you?"

"I reckon not," muttered Sandy. He stood there, intent gaze on King, and something he read in the other man's calm face seemed to reassure him. "All right, boss," he said. "Let's git you into that saddle."

King stood by the buckskin's head, eyes watchful while Sandy helped Garson into the saddle. He had no

intention of giving the cowboy a chance to leap up
behind his boss and make a dash for it.

Sandy seemed to guess his apprehensions, grinned,
shook his head, stepped away from the horse. "No call
to worry," he said acidly. "Ain't claimin' I wouldn't try
it if I had that gun of yours in my holster."

"My good luck at that," smiled King. "Just the same
you can move back a few yards. I'm not taking chances
with you."

"And *I* said you'd no call to worry," complained the
cowboy. He turned, walked over to the big boulder.
"This far enough to suit you?" His smile was hard,
touched with derision.

"Far enough," King said. He chuckled. "I like your
kind at a distance when you're not on my side."

"You've got plenty guts your own self," grinned
Sandy. "Mebbe we'll meet again, feller."

King felt Garson's eyes on him, met his puzzled
stare, and Garson said in an oddly hushed voice, "Keep
wondering where I've seen you before, young man."

"You've never seen me before, Mr. Garson," King
told him, his voice toneless. He swung up behind the
old man. "Get the horse moving, Garson, and
remember, my gun is at your back."

Sandy stood watching, fingers shaping a cigarette,
something akin to wonder and admiration in his eyes.
"Shore has me guessin'," he said aloud. "Cain't figger
him out." He scowled. "Mebbe I'm a damn fool, but
that feller is shore one white man, clean to the bone."
He lit the cigarette, slung canteen to shoulder and
moved doggedly into the chaparral. His high-heeled

boots were not made for walking, but despite an occasional profane comment, his sweat-stained face continued to hold that odd look of wonder.

CHAPTER
EIGHT

Canyon Hideout

Sam Doan halted his horse, sat motionless for long moments, morose gaze fixed on the cattle moving up the dry wash. The moonlight that silvered the landscape showed an oddly dazed look in his eyes. It was obvious that his thoughts vexed him.

There was ample cause for his disquieting apprehensions. He had been a cowman long years and the code of the range was the law by which he judged all men. The code frowned on rustlers and rustling; and now, to his shocked amazement, he was deliberately ignoring that sacred code, was himself a rustler — a low-down cow thief.

He fumbled in his shirt pocket, found a stub of plug tobacco, savagely gnawed off a piece. He had never felt so low in spirit, so bewildered.

A big steer came crashing down the brush-covered slope, whirled at sight of him and galloped to overtake the herd now vanishing around the bend in the canyon. Moonlight showed a sprawling JC on the red hide. Sam winced. Jim Carroll would yell his head off when he discovered that his cows had been rustled.

He continued to wait, gaze on the slope above him, saw a moving shape in the brush. Pete Walker, making a cautious descent, looking for an easy jump down the bluff.

Sam called to him, "Over this way, Pete, where you see that juniper growin' out of a split boulder. There's a wash that levels out easy. Same place your steer hit."

Pete slid his horse down the gravelly wash, pulled alongside, a contented grin on his face. "Doggone that onry hunk of beef," he grumbled. "Come awful close to losin' hisself up thar in the brush." He was as excited and elated as Sam was doleful. "Sure like old times, huh?" he chuckled. "Beats settin' at that damn hotel desk, huh?"

Sam glowered. "Me and you is a couple of weak-minded fools," he told his partner.

"Huh?" Pete eyed him worriedly. "What's eatin' you, Sam, talkin' so gloomy."

"We ain't fit to run loose without hobbles on us," Sam declared. He spat a dark brown stream. "Ain't you got it into your thick haid that me and you has turned cow thieves in our old age?"

"You're loco!" exploded Pete. "We're savin' Jim Carroll's cows for him."

"Jim don't know it," argued Sam. "He's goin' to yell loud that his cows has been rustled." He shook his head. "There's goin' to be ropes danglin' for our necks, old-timer."

Pete felt in his pocket for his plug of tobacco, gnawed it reflectively. "Don't look so good, the way you put it," he admitted. "Doggone it, Sam, I reckon we listened too easy to King's talk."

Sam nodded, trouble heavy on his face. "We ain't knowin' for sure King is on the level," he said.

"Meanin' he's usin' us to help him run off Jim's cows?" asked Pete in a tight voice. "Meanin' he's makin' doggone fools of us?"

Sam frowningly considered the problem, finally shook his head. "I wouldn't claim he's foolin' us," he demurred. "I cain't find it in me to think King is a rustler. His talk about us holding Jim's cows in Bear Creek Canyon listened like good sense. Like I told him, ain't scarcely nobody knows about our place down thar."

"That's right," agreed Pete. His tenseness had left him and the moonlight showed a broad grin on his face. "Only one way to Bear Creek Canyon, and that's whar we're trailin' the herd."

"The way them canyon walls spread out I figger there's more'n five hundred acres in the bowl," pondered Sam. "No way out 'cept where the creek squeezes through. All we got to do is pile plenty brush across the upper gap and them cows has got to stay until time comes to shove 'em out."

"Plenty grass and good water in the creek," added Pete. "I reckon young King has it figgered right." His face sobered. "Some risky for us at that, if Jim Carroll picked up the trail, found his cows hid away in our canyon. Jim's awful short tempered."

His fears made Sam take the opposite view. "I reckon we can leave it to King to handle Jim." He straightened up, confidence back in his eyes. "No need for me and you to worry, Pete, not with young King runnin' this business. He's sure got his grandpa's savvy."

"Got his grandpa's nerve, too," chuckled Pete.

They found King sprawled on a ledge, keeping tally of the cattle as they poured through the gap and went scampering down the slope into the cliff-girded basin.

He got to his feet as they rode up, and the moonlight showed a contented grin on his face.

"Three hundred and twenty-seven, counting that mossyhorn steer you just shoved through, Pete," he called down to them. "That longhorn is sure one old-timer," he added with a chuckle. "I'd say that steer has dodged a lot of roundups."

"He's a doggone outlaw," grumbled Pete. "Did his durndest to break away. Like to have wore my bronc's laigs clean off, chasin' the critter out of the chaparral."

King slid down from the ledge. "Cached my horse back in the scrub," he said. "Be with you in a few minutes."

He was back presently with a silver-maned palomino, and now they rode through the gap, halted again on a bluff that overlooked the basin. The cattle were well down by this time and spreading out.

King relaxed in his saddle, reached into a pocket for tobacco and papers.

"Good horse, Sam," he said. "Lucky for me you keep a few head cached away in this hideout of yours. Ed Yate's buckskin was about played out when I got back to the cabin."

Sam eyed the palomino, and there was pride in the look. "That feller is from old Circle M stock," he told King.

"Can outrun a wolf," declared Pete. "Tough as mesquite."

"Your grandpa got his grandpa from a Mex hidalgo across the border," Sam continued. "Your grandpa was awful smart when it come to sizin' up a horse."

King looked at him, said softly, "And men."

Sam grinned. "Right now he'd figger me for a low-down cow thief." His tone was lugubrious. "Never thought I'd turn rustler in my old age. Makes me feel awful queer."

"Listen to him!" jeered Pete, "and him keepin' it quiet that he's already a hoss thief and that he stole them Circle M colts along with the stud that sired this Silver King you're settin' on right now."

"That wasn't stealin'," Sam defended. "There was plenty pay due us when Circle M was broke up. We took them colts for our pay, you doggone loco maverick." Sam glared at his little partner. "If that's bein' a hoss thief, you can be dangled on the same rope with me."

"He was only joking, Sam," placated King. "You wouldn't steal a hair from a horse's tail unless the horse belonged to you or your outfit." He fingered the rope coiled against his saddle. "You make this one, Sam?"

"Sure did," grinned the old cowman. "That ha'r rope'll hold any steer you ever tie onto." He gave Pete a sidewise glance that held a hint of apology. "Reckon this business has got me some touchy. Ain't likin' it for a fact, son." He shook his head. "Jim Carroll will sure go on the prod when he finds his cows gone from that Mesquite Springs range."

"Carroll would never have seen his cows again if we'd left them at Mesquite," King Malory said dryly. "He's going to be grateful when he learns the truth, knows his herd is cached all safe in your hideout canyon."

"Seems like we should tell him," Sam grumbled. "Awful tough on him, thinkin' his cows has been rustled."

"Mighty tough on Mary, too," worried Pete Walker. "Hate like hell to have the gal grievin', mebbe cryin' her pretty eyes all red."

King made no comment, sat there, his face suddenly hard. If his plans worked, Mary Carroll was surely going to believe the worst of him, unless, and the thought stirred a faint hope in him, unless she maintained unfaltering trust in him. It would be hard for her to hold on to trust, refuse to believe that he was indeed an outlaw, a complete scoundrel.

He said, quietly, "We can't tell Carroll the truth about his cattle. He saw that arrest in San Lucas and recognized me back at Mesquite Springs. He thinks I'm an outlaw and a fugitive from jail. For the present it's important for him to keep on thinking just that. We want the story about me to stick and this business is going to make it stick, get me in touch with the rustler gang we're after."

"I reckon you're talkin' good sense, son," Sam reluctantly agreed. "Jest the same it's awful tough on

Jim. Sure hope I won't be facin' him nor Mary until it's all finished and we got these damn rustlers dancin' on air."

King smiled grimly. "This rustler roundup won't call for ropes and a handy tree," he said. "We'll leave it to the law to handle 'em, once we've got 'em corraled."

Pete spat disgustedly. "Only one way to treat a cow thief," he declared. "Set him to dancin' on air. This here law business don't work any too good."

"That's right," agreed Sam. "They get turned loose because there ain't enough proof, or if they *do* get behind the bars they bust jail or get pardoned and go to prowlin' the range ag'in." He nodded solemnly. "Pete's right, son. Best medicine for a rustler is a rope and a handy tree."

"You fighting old longhorns," laughed King. "I'm betting neither of you ever pulled on a lynch rope in your lives."

Pete began to splutter, subsided as he met Sam's sheepish look. He pretended to choke on his quid, spat it out, gave King a wide grin.

"Waal, young feller," he confessed. "I ain't claimin' you're a liar. Never could brace myself to help swing a rustler nor nobody."

Sam Doan nodded somberly. "That's how come old King Malory was murdered," he reminded. "Swung him from a tree and no chance a-tall for him to prove he was no cow thief." His face hardened and he added sorrowfully, "I reckon old King would likely be alive today if the law had been workin' proper them days."

"There was a lawyer in San Lucas." King Malory's face was a pale mask in the waning moonlight.

"Name of Cole Garson," Pete said harshly.

"He wasn't wantin' no law to hinder *him*," muttered Sam Doan.

They were suddenly wordless, and sat there gazing down at the brooding stillness below. The moon, reaching to the western hills, still gave light enough to show the canyon walls that enclosed the little valley.

It was Sam who broke the silence. "You think that Cole Garson is the man you aim to catch?" he asked softly.

"I don't know." King's tone was thoughtful. "There is a lot of mystery to unravel yet before we get the right answer, Sam."

Pete said practically. "Moon'll soon be down. About time we get the brush piled across the gap."

They loosed their ropes and set to work dragging clumps for the barricade.

CHAPTER
NINE

A Shot from the Chaparral

Jim Carroll stood in the shade of the big cotton-woods grouped around the long watering trough. He was gazing at the ranch buckboard, and there was worry and indecision in his eyes. The wheels were in bad shape, the tires loose, the spokes ready to jump out of their sockets. The tires needed shrinking, and if he delayed much longer the wheels would likely fall apart next time he took a hard drive. It was a job for Tim O'Hara's blacksmith shop in San Lucas. His own ranch forge was useless, the bellows broken and no cash money to buy a new one. For that matter it would mean running up a bill with Tim, and he was still in debt to him for putting a new set of shoes on the team. He hated asking Tim for more credit. Not that Tim would refuse. Tim was big-hearted that way, always willing to wait until a man could pay. The thought that vexed Jim Carroll was the hard fact of his complete inability to pay his bills now or at any time. He was broke, and unless he could hold his steers for the market he would remain broke indefinitely. He could not honorably increase his debt to Tim O'Hara.

The rancher scowled, then came to a decision. Only thing he could do was to get those wheels off and give them a good soaking in the horse trough to swell the dry wood. The treatment would take the rattle out of the spokes and set the tires firm on the rims. He would grease the axles while he was about it.

He dragged trestles from the shed, centered them under the buckboard and raised the vehicle until the wheels cleared the ground.

Mary appeared on the back porch, stood watching him. She wore a pink apron and had a broom in her hand. She looked flushed and hot.

Her father saw her. "Bring me that spanner from the tool box," he called.

She ran down the porch steps and hurried to the shed, found the spanner and took it to him. He set to work removing the wheels.

"Soon as I get them soaking in the trough I'll throw a saddle on Baldy and head for Mesquite Springs," Jim said.

"I wish you wouldn't go," Mary protested. "Garson's men are sure to be there, and you know what he promised he'd do."

"He was bluffing," argued her father. "He's got too much sense to pull off any gunplay, lay himself wide open to a murder charge. He's going to do a lot of loud yellin', but I reckon he'll listen to me and agree to some kind of deal."

Her face clouded. "He'll get the best of the bargain," she worried. "He's got you in a tight place and he knows it."

Jim Carroll slid the wheel from its axle and carried it to the trough. Mary picked up the spanner, began to remove another hubcap. Her father came back from the trough, stood watching her, a frown on his face.

"It's make a deal with him and save what I can, or get out of the cow business," he finally said. "We've got to face the fact that we're broke, Mary. I've been layin' awake all night thinking it over, and I've made up my mind."

She pulled off the hubcap, stepped back for him to remove the wheel, gave him an inquiring look.

"If Garson will let me keep the cows on that Mesquite range until fall, I'm willin' for him to take half of 'em," Carroll said. "It's awful tough, but it's that or nothin'."

"I — I suppose you are right." Her hand lifted in a despondent little gesture, and she went to the other side of the buckboard, set to work on another wheel.

"I'll be back about sundown," Carroll said from the trough. "You give these wheels a turn every once in awhile, Mary. Get 'em soaked up good."

She straightened up from the hubcap, pushed a dark curl from her eyes and gave him a pleading look. "I wish you wouldn't go! The thought frightens me."

"It's make a dicker with him, or starve," Carroll said bluntly.

"There must surely be some other way," insisted Mary. "Ed Yate or that Lestang man. They say Lestang buys and sells cattle."

"You're forgetting something," Carroll told her grimly. "You're forgetting that right now every cow I own is on Mesquite Springs range, and that's why it's make a deal with Cole Garson or nobody. He's got me over a barrel."

Neither of them noticed the several horsemen approaching through the chaparral west of the ranch-yard. Mary bent over the fourth hubcap while her father dumped another wheel into the trough. There was a stubborn look on his face, and it was plain that nothing more she could say would change his purpose.

It was also plain that the riders were using stealth in their approach. Four of them separated, disappeared in the brush. The fifth horseman remained motionless for a few moments, then turned into the avenue that wound through a grove of trees and rode into the yard.

Mary was the first to hear the thud of hoofs. She straightened up from the wheel, brushed at dark curls, eyes widening as she met the rider's smile.

She exclaimed, startled, "Father!"

Carroll swung around from the trough, hand reaching instinctively for his gun. Too late he realized that his gunbelt was on its peg in the house. He stood there, slack-jawed, gazing on Bar G's dark-faced foreman.

Dal Santeen's smile widened, and he said affably, "Hello, folks."

Mary stared at him, the spanner clutched in her hand. She was pale, and there was panic in her golden brown eyes.

Carroll spoke, his voice harsh. "What do you want, Santeen?"

"Makin' a friendly call," grinned the Bar G foreman. His avid look was on the girl. "Wish I'd got here sooner. I'd have helped you take them wheels off."

She repeated her father's question, her voice cold. "What do you want?"

Santeen relaxed in his saddle, produced tobacco and cigarette papers. "Like I said, a friendly call and to tell your pa that the boss craves to hold a palaver with him."

Mary's look went to her father. The disbelief in her eyes failed to impress Carroll. He shook his head at her and something like a relieved smile creased his lined face.

"Garson wants to talk this cow business over, huh, Santeen?" His voice was hopeful.

"That's the idee, Carroll." The Bar G man lit his cigarette, exhaled thin blue smoke. "He wants you over to the ranch for a powwow."

Carroll frowned. "Garson knows where to find me," he said gruffly. "If he wants a powwow he could come see me."

"The boss don't figger it that way." Santeen was watching him carefully now. "You see, Carroll, he wants to know where you took your cows after you got finished waterin' 'em at the springs."

Carroll's face took on a dazed look. He stared, incredulous, disbelieving. His astonishment angered the Bar G foreman.

"No use actin' dumb!" His tone was nasty. "The boss wants to know where you've hid them cows. You tore down his fence, used his water, and played hell with us. He's collectin' plenty damages."

"You're crazy!" Jim Carroll spoke in a hoarse voice. "My JC cows are still on the Mesquite Springs range where I turned 'em loose."

"We've raked every canyon and mesa within five miles of the springs," Santeen told him. "Them cows is gone, and that means you've trailed 'em off some place."

Quick anger now darkened Carroll's face. He made another futile reach for the gun he had left in the house. "It's a trick!" he shouted. "If my cows ain't on that Mesquite range it's because Bar G has rustled 'em."

Santeen shook his head. "We aint touched 'em," he denied. He gave the stricken rancher a hard smile. "If we'd found 'em I wouldn't be here wastin' my time askin' questions." He looked at Mary, added in a quieter voice, "I'm tellin' him the truth."

She said, her voice cold, her eyes unfriendly, "So is Father telling you the truth. We haven't been back to the springs since we left the cattle there night before last."

His expression said that he believed her. He frowned, snubbed his cigarette against saddle horn. "Mighty queer where they got to," he muttered.

Mary was watching her father, an odd apprehension in her eyes. She could read the thoughts now shaping in him, felt no surprise at his next words.

"It's that young feller," he said wrathfully. "He tricked us, Mary."

She said, flatly, "I don't believe it."

"No other answer," fumed her father. "The scoundrel pulled off a smart trick, chasing Garson and his bunch away from there, pretending to help us. He was figuring all along to rustle the herd the moment we headed back to the ranch."

"I don't believe it," Mary repeated.

Santeen said thoughtfully, "The boss told me about that feller." He grinned. "Sure had plenty nerve from what the boss and the boys said about him."

"He's a lowdown cow thief," Carroll declared furiously. "I should have put my gun on him when I had the chance — held him for the sheriff."

"I reckon he's the same feller the Association throwed in jail the other night," Dal Santeen guessed. "Busted out of jail and got clean away."

"That's right," confirmed Carroll. "I saw the arrest, recognized him when he showed up at Mesquite Springs and ambushed your outfit." The rancher hesitated, doubt shadowing his face as he recalled the scene. "I was mighty grateful at the time. That's why I let him ride off, although I did tell him I hated to owe thanks to a cow thief."

"He saved your life," reminded Mary.

Carroll looked at her, silent, distressed, then again anger convulsed his face. "He tricked me!" he shouted.

"Stole my cows! We're ruined, girl! Don't you understand? *Ruined!*"

"You are still alive," Mary said.

"Wasn't hearing this feller's name," Santeen commented. He shrugged, gave Mary an impudent grin. "Too busy havin' a good time over at the Border Palace. Didn't hear about the jail break until next mornin'."

Mary's answering look indicated her complete lack of interest. It was her own private opinion that he had been too drunk to know anything about King Malory or his escape from the San Lucas jail.

Her father said grimly, "Heard him admit to Ed Yate that his name was King Malory. From the talk that went on, he's got a lot of sheriffs looking for him." He gestured fiercely. "Ain't no question about it — he's a rustler, and I'd sure like to get my hands on him."

Santeen's eyes took on an odd glint, and after a moment he said softly, "King Malory, huh. Seems like I heard that name some time back."

"You're going to hear his name plenty more times if we don't get him back in jail mighty quick," declared Carroll.

The Bar G foreman was silent for a moment, his expression thoughtful. "I reckon the boss will want to palaver with you about it," he finally said.

Carroll shook his head. "Ain't got time to waste talking to Garson," he demurred. "I'm heading for town just as quick as I can throw on a saddle."

"The boss said for you to come," insisted Santeen.

"Don't you go with him, Father," Mary advised. She started toward the house. Santeen's gaze followed her trim, graceful figure, his expression suddenly ugly, touched with suspicion.

"What's your hurry?" he called.

She made no answer, but ran up the porch steps. The screen door slammed behind her.

Santeen's look went back to Carroll, and he said almost violently, "Let's get goin'."

The rancher's face reddened. "I told you I'm heading for town. Right now my job is to get the sheriff after this damn rustler. I've got no time to waste on Garson."

Santeen's gun was suddenly in his hand. "The boss sent me to get you." His tone was menacing. "I'm takin' you, Carroll."

Carroll stared at him, growing apprehension in his eyes. The screen door slammed again and Mary's voice broke the momentary hush.

"Drop your gun, Santeen," she said.

The two men turned their heads to look at her. A gun was in her hand, and Carroll recognized his own long-barrelled Colt. He gave the startled Bar G man a triumphant grin that was suddenly an anxious grimace as he saw that Santeen was not inclined to obey the crisp command.

Mary ran down the porch steps, approached swiftly, the gun steady in her hand. Excitement had put color in her cheeks, and it was plain that she meant business.

"I said drop your gun." She halted some ten feet from them, gun leveled straight at Santeen. "I'll shoot," she warned. "I can't miss at this distance."

He only looked at her, something like a malicious grin on his face, and another voice broke the silence, polite, but deadly with its promise of instant death.

"Ma'am, I shore despise to pull trigger on a young gal like you. Jest lower that gun and do it careful."

The color was gone from the girl's face now, leaving it a pale mask. She stole a cautious look at the speaker, recognized him for the man King Malory had set on foot to walk home bootless from Mesquite Springs. Her heart sank as she met the impact of his eyes, the menace of his gun.

"Do what he says, Mary," begged her father. Fear for her made his voice husky.

She obeyed, lowered her gun, stood there rigid with horror as she realized the trap Santeen had set for them.

While the man crouched behind the corral fence kept his gun leveled at her, another man appeared, took the forty-five from her nerveless fingers. Two more men were suddenly in the yard, guns in their hands. One of them halted close behind her father and, at a curt word from Santeen, his companion hurried into the barn.

The Bar G foreman leisurely holstered his gun, a hint of admiration in the grin he gave Mary. "You're sure one little wildcat," he told her. "Was all set to claw me, huh." His laugh was not pleasant to hear. "Tamin' she-wildcats is a chore I like."

"You skunk!" frothed Jim Carroll. He took a quick step, froze to a standstill as he felt the jab of gun barrel against his spine.

Santeen fastened cold eyes on him. "Comin' peaceable, Carroll, or do you want for us to tie you up?"

Carroll's big, gaunt frame sagged dejectedly. He had the look of a sick man, broken by the one last straw his shoulders could not bear.

Mary said contemptuously, eyes blazing at Santeen, "You didn't dare to try it alone, you coward!"

He shrugged, insolence in the smile he gave her. "I'm playin' this hand the best way for him. The boss wasn't wantin' blood spilt. Your pa ain't one to coax with honey." For all his quiet voice, the red in his face showed that her gibe had scored, and as the bitter scorn in her eyes continued to blaze at him, he added angrily, "Keep out of this, ma'am, or you'll be mighty sorry."

Jim Carroll said, his voice a groan. "No more talk from you, Mary. It only makes it worse."

The man who had gone to the barn, appeared with a bald-faced bay horse, saddled and bridled. Mary recognized him now, Sandy Wells, the young cowboy she had danced with at the annual roundup ball, and whose blue eyes had expressed sympathy during the affair at Mesquite Springs.

He did not look at her, but led the horse alongside her father, and stood back with a gesture for Carroll to climb into the saddle.

Dal Santeen said curtly, when Carroll was in the saddle, "Tie his hands loose to the horn, Sandy."

The man obeyed, but Mary read animosity in the brief glance he gave the Bar G foreman. It was plain to her that Sandy had no love for Santeen, and was not liking this dark business — a vagrant thought from which she tried to squeeze some hope.

Santeen spoke again, "All right, boys. Get your broncs."

The men hurried away to their concealed horses. Santeen slouched at ease in his saddle, fingers busy with tobacco and cigarette papers.

Mary broke the tense silence. "I want to go with you," she said.

Her father shook his head. "Won't help matters, you coming."

Self-control was at the breaking point. Her mouth trembled. "I — I'm afraid for you —"

He tried to reassure her. "I reckon Garson only wants to talk things over, like Santeen says."

"I'm afraid," she repeated. "Dreadfully afraid."

Santeen broke into the conversation. "No harm in her comin' if she wants to ride along with us."

The smirk on the man's dark face frightened her, made her instantly abandon the plan. After all, she would be powerless to help her father once they were at the Garson ranch. It would be sheer folly to go, and further complicate the situation. Dal Santeen was dangerous. Her continued disdain of his attentions seemed only to inflame him. He would stop at nothing to have his way with her.

Her thoughts ran like a swift, cool current now, made her see clearly that she must keep her freedom to act. She must get to town as fast as she could, seek help there, tell her story to Sam Doan and Ed Yate.

Her father spoke again, misinterpreting the set, hard look of her. "I'm not letting you go along with us to Garson," he said harshly. "You stay at home here."

She was glad now of his insistence. She could pretend to surrender, allay any suspicions that Santeen might have.

"All right," she forced reluctance into her voice, "if that's the way you feel."

"I do," Jim Carroll told her gruffly. "You stay here and mind the house."

The four Bar G men rode into the avenue from the concealing brush. Dal Santeen said, "Let's go. You in front of me, Carroll."

Mary watched, her heart torn by the gray look on her father's face. She read despair there, a lack of hope that sent a shiver through her. Perhaps she would never see him again alive. She began to tremble, resisted the impulse to run after him and kiss him good-bye. It would be too much for him, and for her. She would break down and they would take him away, leaving her there in futile tears.

The chaparral hid them from view. She shook off her daze. It was time for action now. Every minute was precious, not to be wasted by weakening, fear-ridden thoughts. She ran into the barn, dragged her saddle from its peg and hurriedly threw it on the chestnut mare. No time to lose. *No time to lose.* The thought hammered at her, kept her mind and fingers steady as she jerked the cinch tight, drew on the bridle. She must hold onto her courage, keep her wits working.

She sprang into the saddle, rode the mare at a gallop to the back porch, slid down and ran into the house to change into her blue jeans. Long skirts would hamper the hard ride to San Lucas. She failed to notice the lone horseman turning into the avenue.

In something less than ten minutes she was running down the porch steps to the waiting mare, one hand pulling on a white felt hat, her other hand pushing three silver dollars into a pocket of her jeans. Her booted foot lifted to stirrup and, as she hit the saddle, she whirled the mare and headed for the avenue.

What she saw as she tore around the house made her pull the mare to a plunging standstill. She wanted to scream, could only stare with sick eyes at the horseman waiting there.

Santeen smiled, spoke softly. "Looks like you're goin' some place in a hurry."

Mary could find no words. Her heart was hammering, her body limp. She felt as helpless as any rabbit under the death swoop of a hawk.

"Figgered you was mebbe headin' for town," Santeen said, his voice hard now.

She forced herself to speak. "Let me pass!"

He shook his head, smile widening. "I got other idees for you, honey gal."

Courage was hardening in her again now that the horror of surprise was over. "I should have killed you when I had the chance." She flung the words fiercely. "There should be a bounty on wolves like you."

Mirth rocked him in the saddle. "I like 'em plenty spirited, gal." He swung his horse, hand reaching for her bridle rein. She tried to swerve the mare aside and suddenly Santeen's horse squealed, went into the air, back humped in a frenzy of bucking. Taken unawares, and off balance, Santeen pitched headlong from his saddle, landed with a crash in a clump of buckthorn. The horse broke into a gallop, vanished into the chaparral.

Mary wasted no time getting away, sent the mare into a run down the avenue. She only knew that somebody concealed in the cottonwoods had taken a shot at Santeen and that the bullet must have grazed his horse. She wondered wildly if her unseen deliverer could have been King Malory.

She tore around the next bend, glimpsed a lone rider and knew that her guess was wrong. Her rescuer was Sandy. He gestured violently for her to keep going, swung his horse into a ravine and disappeared.

It was very confusing. Sandy Wells was a Bar G man, and Santeen his boss. Only one thing stood clear. The blond young cowboy was a friend for some mysterious reason, and had proved himself a man. There was decency in him.

A great gratitude welled in her. The thing had been too dreadfully close.

Mary drew the mare to a fast running walk. She was beyond danger of pursuit now, and it was senseless to gallop the mare off her feet. It was a long way yet to San Lucas.

CHAPTER
TEN

King Malory Makes a Call

The gate was open. King rode into the yard, saw a long hitch rail under a line of big chinaberry trees. There was a windmill there and a long trough. Shade and water was what he wanted for his horse. He turned in that direction, slid from his saddle and let his horse drink sparingly before tying him to the rail. He was using the buckskin for this visit to Cole Garson's home ranch. The palomino might arouse dangerous curiosity, and betray his secret friendship with Sam Doan and Pete Walker. Such a disclosure would be unfortunate at this time.

He was grimly aware of the risk he was incurring, accepting Cole Garson's invitation: Sam and Pete had maintained that he was walking into a trap, been skeptical of Garson's promise not to harm him. It was necessary to mend his fences where Garson was concerned. The beginning had been unfortunate, but he had done considerable repair by riding the old man home to the ranch. Garson had been surprisingly grateful, announced bluntly that King would find it

103

profitable to have a talk with him. Despite the affair at Mesquite Springs he liked King and could use a man with his kind of nerve.

The stillness in the big ranchyard aroused a growing uneasiness. The quiet was ominous. He had the uncomfortable feeling that eyes were watching him.

He stood there, wary now as he studied his surroundings. It was apparent that Cole Garson did things in a big way. The barns were enormous, the corrals large, the fences well built. Another windmill stood near the main barn, and a big tank. Midway between the barn and the high hedge that surrounded the rambling ranch house was a long, low building half hidden in a grove of cottonwood trees. The bunkhouse, King decided, and strangely lifeless at this moment.

Impatient with himself for his vague alarms, he walked to the gate in the hedge, pushed it open and stepped into the garden.

A voice said, softly, "Hold it, feller."

King became very still; and now he saw the speaker, standing close to the hedge, gun leveled. He sensed other eyes on him, turned his head in a look, met the hard grin from a second man pressed close to the hedge.

The first speaker's voice came again. "Take it easy and there'll be no trouble. All we want is your gun, and then you can walk right in and see the boss."

"I'm keeping my gun," King said.

"That's up to you, mister," the man said. "If you ain't givin' up your gun you can go fork your bronc and ride away from here. You don't go into the house with that gun on you."

"Garson asked me to come," King argued.

The man shook his head. "Nobody gets to the boss with a gun on him."

King looked at him, then looked at the other man. He had never seen them before. They had not been among those present at the Mesquite Springs affair. He read no animosity in their faces, only determination not to let him pass unless he surrendered his gun.

A high, thin voice broke the stillness, drew King's look to the long, sprawling house set back in the trees. Cole Garson stood there, on the porch, a vaguely seen black shape in the shadows.

"Let him keep his gun, Cisco," the rancher called out. "Bring him into the office." He turned away, vanished into the house.

Cisco gave King a nod. "All right, feller. You heard him."

King walked up the path, mounted the porch steps. The two men followed close on his heels. A glance told him they were watchful, their guns ready.

A door stood open. He heard Cisco's toneless voice. "Go right in, mister."

Cole Garson watched them, his beady eyes sharp and probing. The big leather chair with its high back made him seem even smaller, and now that he was without his hat, King saw that his flattish skull was entirely bald. He looked more than ever like a buzzard with his beak of a nose and watchful, obsidian eyes.

His hand lifted in a gesture, and the two men moved across the room and disappeared through another door. His hand moved again, pointed to a chair opposite him. King sat down, waited for him to speak.

"So you decided to come," Garson said. "Weren't you afraid, young man?"

"I had your word there'd be no trouble," King reminded.

"You wouldn't give up your gun," Garson said.

"Why should I?" King smiled. "That wasn't in the bargain."

"I don't wear a gun myself," Garson told him. "I don't like my guests to feel they must be armed when they visit me."

"You can hardly call me a guest," King said bluntly. He gazed around curiously, marveling a bit as he took in the appointments of the big room. Not much resemblance here to the usual ranch office. The high ceiling was beamed with lustrous, peeled logs of yellow pine, and fine Navajo rugs covered the floor. There were paintings on the walls, rich draperies, a great bookcase filled with leather-bound law books. The desk was a heavy table of polished, dark wood. An ancient piece from old Mexico, King guessed. A great crystal chandelier hung from the ceiling. Another piece from some hidalgo's hacienda. Two large windows, with wide glass doors between, overlooked a high-walled garden gay with flowers. A Mexican peon in white cotton drawers and tall steeple hat made indolent motions with a hoe, cigarette drooping from his lips.

King felt Garson's eyes on him. He grinned. "For a cowman, I'd say you like luxury and comfort," he drawled.

"Yes." Garson lifted a clawlike hand. "Also security, as you will see, young man, if you will look more closely."

King looked in the indicated direction, froze in his chair as he caught the glint of two rifle barrels protruding from an opening in the wall where a panel had silently slid back. Cisco and his companion were still very much on guard.

"You see now why I was willing for you to keep your gun, young man," Garson continued, a hint of amusement in his thin, dry voice. "You have already taught me the wisdom of not taking chances with you."

King was silent. He wanted to be rid of the cold prickles along his spine. Careful to keep his hands in view of the men behind the rifle barrels, he fished tobacco sack and papers from his shirt pocket and slowly built a cigarette.

"You hurt my feelings, Mr. Garson," he finally murmured. He put a match to the cigarette, and gave his host a reproachful grin.

"I wanted to make sure you understood." The sharp little eyes were watching him intently. "It would have pained me if any rashness on your part too abruptly terminated our interview."

"You don't talk like an ordinary run-of-the-mill cowman," commented King. He gestured at the tall bookcase. "I'd say those are law books from the look of 'em."

"I was once a lawyer," Garson told him, his unwinking eyes probing hard now. "I chose to abandon the law for the life of a cattleman." He paused, added softly, "I am a successful cattleman, *Mr. Kingman Malory.*"

Cold prickles again chased up and down King's spine. Not the chill warning of imminent disaster. It was exultation that stirred in him, a realization that his decision to save this man from almost certain death in the desert was bearing the fruit he yearned to pick.

He said, his voice low, "You seem to know my name."

Garson's unpleasant hairless head moved in a hardly perceptible confirming nod. "The news of King Malory's arrest in San Lucas and his break from jail has reached me." He paused, gaze intent on the younger man. "I think I told you that your face seemed oddly familiar. You are very like my partner of the long years ago. It is possible you are his grandson."

King nodded, waited for him to continue.

"A tragic affair," Garson continued, a faraway look now in his eyes. "No doubt the details of his untimely death are well known to you, Mr. Malory."

King was careful to keep his eyes away from the menacing rifle barrels. The crisis demanded that he use caution. Garson had learned that a notorious outlaw named King Malory had escaped from the San Lucas jail. The name, the likeness, had convinced him of the kinship to old King Malory. The odds were against his knowing anything more. Cole Garson really believed

108

the story of his outlawry, and it was obvious that he found the story interesting.

He heard his own voice, husky, not quite steady. "I was awfully young at the time, Mr. Garson. I — I never knew what to believe."

"A tragic affair," repeated Garson. He leaned back in the great chair, hairless-lidded eyes narrowed to slits. "You wouldn't be knowing much, and the years have been many since it happened."

King was aware of tightening muscles. He wanted to leap on this man, clasp hard fingers over the skinny throat. It was Garson who was responsible for the rope that had strangled old King Malory to death.

He struggled out of his rage, said tonelessly, "You know I'm a rustler, Mr. Garson. A fugitive from the law."

"Ed Yate so charges." The owner of Bar G smiled for the first time. "As a member of the Stockmen's Association I should have no sympathy for your breed. As a friend of your long-dead grandfather, my one-time partner, I confess to a weakness — a wish to help you out of this sad predicament."

"Ed Yate might make it tough for you, helping a rustler." King gave him a wry smile. "Why should you want to help me, Mr. Garson?" His smile widened. "I was mighty rough with you and your outfit at Mesquite Springs the other day."

Cole Garson's eyes were boring gimlets. "I don't need explanations about that affair. Jim Carroll is a cow thief, which explains why you helped him." He went on, not waiting for a reply, "I have a second reason for wishing to help you, young man. You turned us loose to make a terrible walk home to this ranch. I could not have survived the ordeal. You could have left me to a most unpleasant death. I am grateful that you did not, and am disposed to offer you my protection."

"It won't be easy hiding me out from the sheriff," King said dryly.

"You admit then that you are a rustler?" Garson asked the question softly.

"That's the talk," smiled King. He shrugged. "I'm not admitting anything."

"You can be frank with me," urged the old man. "I can keep you safe from the law. My ranch is large, and I can use a good cowman. We'll forget that your name is King Malory." He paused, studied King thoughtfully. "I had a young nephew who died years ago. His name was Phil Cole. You can take his name, be this nephew, perhaps someday be my heir."

"It won't be easy fooling Ed Yate or the U. S. deputy marshal if they laid eyes on me," argued King.

"We can change your looks some," Garson said. "A beard would do the trick. We'll keep you undercover until you've grown a good beard."

"Mighty risky," objected King. "Best thing for me to do is head a long way from this San Lucas country."

Garson showed annoyance. "You're a fool to keep on the dodge when you can have security right here on my ranch."

King's glance idled around the big, handsome room. "And comfort and luxury," he commented musingly. He smiled at the old man opposite him. "Sounds

110

mighty good, Mr. Garson. I'll have to do some hard thinking about it." He got out of the chair. "Thanks for the powwow."

"Don't be a fool, young man." Garson's tone showed a growing impatience. "Your decision must be made now."

King was suddenly acutely aware of danger in that room. Whatever his decision, he was already a prisoner. Garson would not let him leave the place alive.

An ash tray, fashioned from a piece of polished steer horn and trimmed with silver, stood on the table Garson used for a desk. King snubbed his cigarette in it and dropped the stub. He did it carefully, conscious of the menacing rifle barrels. He wanted time to think it over. It was quite possible that Garson was the secret leader of the rustler gang. Acceptance of his offer would mean an amazing opportunity to unmask him. A risky business and dark with unpleasant possibilities for an amateur range detective.

It was not fear for himself that worried him. Dangerous moments were unavoidable in this job as secret investigator for the San Lucas Stockmen's Association. What *did* worry him was the fear of failure. There was more to this job than merely wiping out a gang of rustlers and securing evidence against the ringleader. He had a personal reason, a solemn vow to unearth from dark years the story of a murder, and bring the murderer to justice.

It was Sam Doan's theory that Garson was the murderer of King's grandfather. King was not yet convinced. He would need more proof. One thing was certain — Garson was up to no good. He knew now that King was his former partner's grandson and, therefore, potentially dangerous. If he had killed once, he would not hesitate to kill again if he suspected the real purpose that had brought King to San Lucas. It was plain that Garson was not certain that King had any suspicions. He really believed that King was a rustler — an outlaw on the dodge. The thought would please him. Once King was a member of the Bar G outfit, Garson's knowledge would be a useful club to enforce obedience and guarantee his loyalty. In the meantime, he would have King under his eyes and be able to study him. If things went wrong the dead body of a wanted outlaw would be turned over to the sheriff. Garson would make sure that King did not live long enough to endanger the security of Bar G's owner.

Garson said fretfully, "Make up your mind, young man."

King held onto his careless grin. "I'd feel a lot safer back in the Panhandle." He shook his head. "Seems like you'll be taking a big risk hiding me out from the law."

"That's my worry," Garson snapped.

"I reckon you're right at that." King's covert glance told him the rifle barrels were still there, but sagging somewhat out of line now. Cisco and his companion were obviously too confident, inclined to be careless.

His fingers itched to clamp hard on the butt of the gun in his holster. He dared not make the downward reach. Two pairs of eyes were watching his hands. A wrong movement would bring death blasting from those rifles.

His look lowered to the ash tray on the table. No good for a weapon, but a possible means of causing a diversion. He wanted to get down on the floor, with that massive table a barricade at his back.

He said, casually, "Mighty nice tray you got carved out of that steer horn." His left hand moved toward it as he spoke, and suddenly he was on the floor, his other hand jerking the gun from holster.

The brief silence was broken by Cisco's startled voice. "Cain't see him for the table!"

King heard the hurried tramp of booted feet. He said fiercely to Garson, leaning back in the big chair, face ashen, "Call off your dogs!"

Garson's horrified eyes were fastened on the menacing gun less than a yard from his stomach. His voice came, the agonized squeal of a frightened rabbit. "Stop! He'll kill me if you don't keep back."

The rush of booted feet hushed, and again there was silence, disturbed only by Garson's rasping breath. Outside in the gay little flower garden the Mexican peon leaned on his shovel, gazed curiously at the two men in the doorway, rifles clutched in their hands.

King spoke again. "Get up!" He motioned with his gun. "Stand in front of me and keep your hands high."

Garson got out of the chair, lifted trembling hands, let out a stifled moan as King stepped behind him and pressed the gun against his back.

"I want those men in here where I can see them," King said.

Fear of instant death made Garson eager to obey, and at his croaking command the two men leaned their rifles against the wall, slowly approached, hands lifted above their heads. They were a dazed-looking pair. King looked them over carefully. He would have to get possession of the six guns still in their holsters. He had caught a bear by the tail, and the least mistake meant sure disaster.

The Mexican in the garden still leaned on his shovel and suspicion was plain on his swarthy face now. It was equally plain that he was reluctant to mix into the affairs of these Americanos.

The sight of him out there worried King. He said to Garson, "Call that man in here, and watch your tongue." The prod of his gun emphasized the warning.

Garson's first panic was subsiding. His voice lifted in a sharp command. "Manuel, come quick!"

The Mexican drove the shovel into soft earth with a thrust of his foot and slouched up the path and into the room. He halted abrutly, stared with frightened eyes. King guessed that in the darkened room he must have been invisible to Manuel out in the bright sunlight. The Mexican's curiosity had merely been aroused by the sight of the two armed men running to the office door. Surprise, dismay held him rigid.

Kicking himself for allowing a false alarm to increase the odds against him, King addressed the man in Spanish. "Obey, and you will not be hurt."

Manuel rolled scared eyes at his boss, saw no help there. "*Si, señor,*" he muttered.

"Get over there behind those men. Take their guns and put them on the table by me."

The Mexican looked again at Garson, who said huskily, "Obey, fool, or he will kill me!"

Manuel sidled behind the men, secured their guns and laid both weapons on the table.

"Get down on your bellies," King now ordered the sullen prisoners.

The jab of gun barrel against his spine drew a gasp from Garson. He repeated frantically, "Obey, fools!"

Cisco and his companion stretched face down on the floor. King spoke again to the Mexican who awkwardly removed the men's cartridge belts and placed them near the guns on the table.

"Tie them up," King said to him in Spanish. He gestured at the cords that held the window draperies. "Make a good job of it, or you'll be sorry."

Manuel did not waste time in more appealing looks at his boss. This terrible Americano flashed lightning from his eyes when he talked. He meant business.

"*Si, si, señor.*" The Mexican snatched the tough cords from the hanging and set to work. His two victims cursed him while he bound arms and legs and drew the knots tight.

"I'll cut your heart out, you damn Mex," Cisco promised.

Manuel finished the job, stood up and gave King a worried look. "They will kill me," he said in Spanish. "You must not leave me here to die."

"We will leave this place together," reassured King.

"*Gracias.*" Manuel's brown face showed quick relief. He looked questioningly at Garson, caught King's gesture, and jerked another cord from its silk hanging.

Cole Garson said furiously, "You'll be sorry for this, young man."

"Your own fault," gibed Cisco from the floor. "You wouldn't let us take his gun when we had the chance."

"Shut up!" rasped his boss. "Wouldn't have happened if you two had kept better watch."

"You can sit down in your chair, Mr. Garson," smiled King. "We'll make it easy for you."

Garson sank into the leather cushion and the Mexican swiftly tied his ankles to the front legs of the chair, looped the rope over a wrist, passed the rope under the chair and made it fast to the other wrist.

King nodded his satisfaction. Manuel was handy with a rope and knew how to tie a good knot.

"You'll be sorry," repeated Garson. "You can't get away with it, Malory."

"Your own fault," King told him. "I came in peace at your invitation. You chose to set your hired killers on me." His voice hardened. "You had no intention of letting me leave here alive." He waggled his gun at the rancher. "You got frightened when you learned my name. You didn't like the idea of King Malory's grandson running loose in the San Lucas country."

"You're crazy!" Garson's face was the color of dirty parchment. "I don't know what you mean."

King stared at him, his eyes cold. "I think you do, Mr. Garson." He gave the Mexican a look. "Tie up his mouth."

Manuel gagged the three prisoners, using their own bandannas on Cisco and his companion. Garson's handkerchief was too small and the Mexican drew out

116

a long knife from inside his cotton shirt, deftly sliced a black silk sleeve from Garson's arm. The malice in the Mexican's eyes as he gagged his boss told King that the man was thinking of numerous indignities he had received from the owner of Bar G ranch.

"*Está bien. Vamos.*" King picked up the confiscated guns and belts, motioned for Manuel to precede him to the wide, front porch. He paused for a cautious look. The garden was clear. Nobody in sight, and now they went swiftly to the gate where the two Bar G men had waited in ambush for him.

He halted again for a careful scrutiny of the big ranchyard. The stillness there puzzled him, aroused apprehensions of another ambush.

Manuel read his thoughts, shook his head. "Only the choreman is here," he said in Spanish. "The vaqueros rode away with Señor Santeen, early this morning."

King motioned him through the gate. He was not yet quite sure of the Mexican, and had no desire to feel a knife suddenly in his back.

They reached the buckskin horse drooping at the hitch rail near the water trough. King glanced at the gun-filled belts in his hand, hesitated, looked at the Mexican who grinned, shook his head, patted the knife now back inside his shirt. The gesture was enough. Manuel had no wish for a gun. His knife was the weapon he preferred.

King's arm lifted in a swing that sent guns and belts into the horse trough. He turned to the buckskin, hesitated again, his look on the Mexican.

"You have a horse?" he asked.

"No, señor."

"Grab one from the barn," King suggested.

Manuel shook his head. "I do not wish to be hung for a horse thief," he explained in Spanish. He gestured. "*Por la cruz*, I would not last long."

King was worried. He had plunged this man into a serious predicament. "You can't stay here," he said, "and you won't get far on foot."

"It is very bad," Manuel agreed unhappily. "If Cisco catches me, I will die full of his bullets, or hang from a tree."

"You've got to get away from here even if it means stealing a horse," King said, his voice grim.

"I will not steal a horse." The Mexican's tone was stubborn. He added nervously. "We must get away from this place fast. The vaqueros may return and then, *por Dios!*" He gestured, lifted an expressive shoulder.

A man appeared in the entrance to the main barn, stood watching them, a pitchfork in his hand.

Manuel whispered, "*The choreman.*" He seized the lead rope, made a show of fastening it to the saddle. The man moved on with his pitchfork, disappeared behind a long strawpile.

"Quick!" implored the Mexican.

King was suddenly in the saddle. "Climb up behind," he said.

They rode across the yard and through the wide-open gate; and now beyond view, King sent the horse into a run.

CHAPTER
ELEVEN

Trail to Danger

A trail cut eastward from the ranch road. King followed it, worked his way down a brush-covered slope to the floor of a canyon and halted the horse inside a small clearing some score yards above the trail. This was new country, and he had left the Bar G ranch in a hurry. He wanted to get his bearings and he wanted to come to a decision about his new ally.

Just what to do with Manuel had him puzzled. There were reasons why he could not take him to the Bear Canyon hideout. For one thing, he suspected that Sam Doan would not like it. Also, he was reluctant to let the Mexican know too much about himself. He had taken a liking for the man, sensed integrity in him. He might prove useful.

Manuel slid from the horse and stood watching him, a curious mingling of admiration and anxiety in his brown eyes. He said softly, almost to himself, "*Un caballero grande.*"

King grinned, got down from his saddle and found a boulder.

"You are glad to get away from that place?" he asked in Spanish.

Manuel nodded. "He would not let me go. I owed him much money, he would say. A lie. I work it out, but he would always say I owe him money. He is a devil."

"He must not catch you," King said. "Where can you go to be safe from him?"

"There is one place where I will be safe," Manuel told him. "I will go back to Los Higos below the border. My uncle, Francisco Cota, has a *cantina*. I will go to him."

"A long walk," commented King.

Manuel shrugged. "A man walks when he has no horse."

"We must think of some plan to get you back to Los Higos," King said. He was silent for a long moment. The Mexican stirred uneasily under his penetrating stare.

"Your eyes ask questions," he finally muttered.

"You've seen a lot that goes on at that ranch," King guessed. "From that little back garden you have seen those who visit Garson."

"Not many," answered Manuel. "Sometimes there are men who come there." He shook his head. "I do not know them."

"You would know them again if you saw them?" King questioned.

The Mexican nodded. "One who sometimes comes is very grand and wears a black mustache with wax on it. Once he threw me a silver dollar."

King's brows furrowed thoughtfully. The description meant nothing to him, but he would keep it in mind. "Anybody else you remember?"

Manuel took off his steeple hat, rubbed his thick black hair reflectively. "There is one who comes," he finally recalled, "a tall man with gray in his hair. A stern one who speaks with authority, like one who is rich. Señor Garson talks polite to this one. I think he fears him."

"You don't know his name?"

Manuel shook his head. He was studying the big buckskin. His brown hand lifted in a gesture at the horse. "This one is like the buckskin horse the gray one was riding the last time he make the visit."

King's look went to the horse. He was startled, vaguely alarmed. The buckskin was the horse supplied for his escape from the San Lucas jail. He had not inquired about the owner. Ed Yate had merely said he would find a horse cached in the chaparral.

King scowled and shook his head impatiently. The thing was impossible. His eyes went suddenly hard. Perhaps not too impossible. He must ask Sam Doan about the ownership of the buckskin so like the one used by Manuel's mysterious *rico*.

He gave the Mexican a kindly look. "I'll get you back to Los Higos," he promised again. "I'll want you to stay at the *cantina* of your uncle, Francisco Cota, until I come to see you."

"*Si, señor,*" acquiesced the Mexican. "*Por la cruz,* I will stay. I am your man."

King fumbled in a pocket, drew out two gold pieces. "Take these now," he said. "Serve me well and you will have more."

"*Por Dios!*" exulted the Mexican. "Such gold has never before been mine all at one time. I was already your man. Now I am your eyes, your ears —"

"And my good friend," smiled King.

"I will not wait for a horse to carry me to Los Higos," Manuel declared. "*Verdad!* I go now, for this gold has put wings on my feet. The miles to the border will be nothing for one whose pockets are lined with such bright gold."

King's hand lifted for silence. He was gazing intently at the trail below.

"Somebody comes," he whispered. He drew his gun, crouched there, continued to watch. Manuel slid his knife from his cotton shirt, bent low by his side. King was pleased. The Mexican had courage.

Stones rattled under approaching hoofs, and the horse was suddenly in view under their eyes. No rider sat in the saddle and the reins were dangling.

King listened for a moment, heard no other sound. The riderless horse was alone. He gave Manuel a brief grin, went angling down the slope and cut into the trail. The horse saw him too late, tried to swerve aside. King grabbed the dangling reins, held on, brought him to a halt.

He led the animal up to the clearing, said laconically, "You don't need to make that trip to Los Higos on foot, Manuel."

The Mexican stared big-eyed at the roan. "*Por Dios,*" he muttered. "Señor Santeen's horse, that one." He shook his head. "No, no, señor. He will kill me if I take that horse."

"He won't know anything about it," King said. "He's somewhere back on the trail, dead perhaps, from the look of that bullet wound." He pointed at the red streak on the roan's withers. "Been some shooting."

Manuel's eyes glinted as he thought it over. "The news of his death would be music," he said simply.

"You do not like him?"

"He is bad, a mad wolf," declared the Mexican.

"You say he went off with the vaqueros early this morning?" King asked.

Manuel nodded. "Some place known as Mesquite Springs."

Worry filled King's eyes as he continued to stare at the riderless horse. *Mesquite Springs*. It began to seem possible that the Bar G man had run into Jim Carroll. The salty old JC man would have had small chance against Santeen's riders.

King stifled a groan, gaze still on the ominous red streak. One thing was certain. Jim Carroll had done some shooting, evidently knocked the Bar G foreman from his saddle. The wounded, riderless horse told a grim story of battle.

He motioned to the empty saddle. "Climb up, Manuel. Get going for Los Higos. Keep out of sight and turn the horse loose this side of the border."

Manuel crawled into the saddle. "I will wait for you at the *cantina* of my uncle, Francisco Cota," he promised.

"Avoid the trails," King warned.

"I will be a coyote for cunning," grinned the Mexican.

King watched him disappear in the chaparral. The problem of getting Manuel Cota across the border had been solved in a strange manner.

The presence here of Santeen's riderless horse puzzled him. He got out Sam Doan's map and, as he suspected, found that he was in Borrego Canyon which ran considerably south of Mesquite Springs.

He stuffed the map back in his pocket, worry in his eyes as he recalled Manuel's words. *He went off early this morning. Some place known as Mesquite Springs.* It was plain that Garson had sent the outfit to round up the JC cattle. The disappearance of the herd must have puzzled the Bar G foreman. He would jump to the conclusion that Carroll had trailed the herd back to his own ranch.

King was appalled. Santeen had gone to the Carroll ranch. The wounded riderless horse was proof of serious trouble there. No telling what might have happened. Old Jim Carroll was not one to be pushed around. He would go for his gun.

One thing was certain. Mary was in grave danger. The thought chilled King. He swung into his saddle and sent the buckskin down to the trail.

Despite his anxiety to make speed he knew that caution was necessary. The chances were good that the Bar G men were not far away. He must see them before they saw him.

Watchful, ears alert for warning sounds, he kept the horse down to a slow walk, avoided stones that would rattle under shod hoofs, paused at each bend in the trail to listen.

A buzzard suddenly lifted into view with a frantic flapping of wings. King reined his horse. The sound was unmistakable. Horsemen approaching.

He rode into the scrub and tied the horse to a tough root. He wanted a close look, crawled to a clump of bushes a few yards from the trail.

They came on around the bend, six riders in single formation. The faces of the first two were unfamiliar. The third man, on a bald-faced horse, was Jim Carroll, his hands tied to saddle horn.

The fourth rider, a tall, swarthy man with an arm carried in an improvised sling, King guessed must be Santeen, the Bar G foreman. Trailing the cattle boss was the man he had set on foot at Mesquite Springs.

The last of the riders drew close. His head turned in a careless glance at the clump of bushes. King recognized the cowboy he knew as Sandy. He held his breath, tightened fingers over gun butt. For a chilling moment he thought Sandy had looked right into his eyes, stiffened perceptibly in his saddle.

They drifted past, a strangely silent, morose crew. It was plain that failure to locate the JC cattle had put them in a sour mood.

King watched them, his face grim, his heart heavy with forebodings. Enraged by the mystery of the vanished herd, Santeen was taking Jim Carroll to Bar G for questioning by Cole Garson. The outlook was more than unpleasant for Carroll. He would not know the answers, unless by now he suspected the notorious outlaw who had escaped from the San Lucas jail. It was possible he might convince Garson that it was King Malory who had stolen the herd.

The thing had been too uncomfortably close, King reflected. He had made his escape from Bar G in the nick of time. Garson would have stopped at nothing to make him divulge the whereabouts of the herd. In any event, he would soon have put an end to the man whose purpose in the San Lucas country he had good reason to fear.

King got to his feet, took a cautious look up the canyon. The riders were beyond the upper bend now, and the faint haze of dust indicated they had turned up the slope where the trail forked west to the mesa. Less than an hour would see their arrival at the ranch.

He returned to his horse, stood irresolute, his thoughts churning. One thing seemed clear. The raiders had not found Mary Carroll at home, or else she had managed to elude capture. He felt that she was safe for the moment.

Her father was the immediate problem. Garson had no liking for Jim Carroll. There was bad blood between the two men. Carroll had bluntly accused the Bar G man of deliberately trying to ruin him, which was probably the truth. Garson wanted the Carroll ranch. There was no shred of scruple in the man. He would not hesitate to remove Carroll from the scene.

King stared bleakly at the lifting haze of dust. Jim Carroll's life was in peril. He would dangle from a tree, choke to death at the end of a rope, and the story would spread that he was a cow thief caught in the act. Cole Garson's cunning would make sure of the proof. Another man safely murdered as he had murdered once before in the long years ago. And like an echo of that same past, forged papers would make him the owner of the coveted JC range.

The wind freshened, made sighing sounds in the brush. King stirred, restless under the lash of his thoughts. He was partly responsible for the grim tragedy that threatened Mary Carroll's father. His plan to save the JC herd had boomeranged. If he had left the cattle alone Santeen would have found them and Jim Carroll would not now be helpless in Garson's hands. At the worst Carroll would have had a chance to make some kind of a deal with Garson, sell him the ranch for at least enough cash to enable him to get out of the country.

King turned to his horse. He had no alternative. It was up to him to do something. He could never again face Mary Carroll if he failed her father at this desperate time.

The west slope was in shadow when he reached the trail that looped up to the mesa. He let the horse take the climb at a leisurely walk. He would need the cover of darkness when he reached the Bar G ranch and he had plenty of time.

The shadows deepened, drew a darkening veil over the floor of the canyon below. The stillness was complete. Only the creak of his own saddle leathers, the crunch of the buckskin's shod hoofs.

He reached the rimrock where the trail twisted between tumbled boulders. The sun was behind the mountains now, the yellow light fading. It was still too early in the evening to suit his purpose.

King halted the horse, slid from saddle and felt in a pocket for his tobacco sack. The buckskin took a step toward some bunch grass, began to nibble. King watched him, fingers busy shaping his cigarette.

For some reason, uneasiness suddenly seized him. He made no attempt to lift his head in a look, continued as he was, apparently preoccupied with the cigarette. He put the cigarette between his lips, made a show of feeling in his pockets for a match; and now his sharpened ears heard what he was waiting for, a whisper of movement in the sagebrush.

He went down in a twisting roll that landed him behind a boulder. A dry branch of buckthorn snapped under his weight, a sharp crackle of sound that made the buckskin jump.

King lay there, reached for his gun and took a cautious look. Relief surged through him. The buckskin was over his momentary panic, was again nosing at the bunch grass.

The minutes dragged and it was very still there. Only the buckskin nosing at the grass. The yellow twilight deepened to a soft purple.

A voice cut through the silence. "I'm cravin' peace talk, mister."

It was a voice King had heard before. He had *not* been mistaken. Sandy had seen him crouched behind the bush down on the lower trail. For some mysterious reason he had chosen to ride on, and say nothing to Santeen.

The cowboy's purpose in dropping back for this lone ambush puzzled King. Or was it a lone ambush? For all he knew, the bushes were alive with Bar G men.

His own voice now broke the silence. "Are you alone?"

"Wouldn't be no peace talk if I wasn't alone," Sandy answered.

"What do you want?"

"Ain't nothin' I want save a powwow with you."

"If I'd ridden another ten yards you'd have emptied your gun into me," King accused. "Stopping back here spoiled your ambush."

"I figgered you'd listen to my talk some better if I had a gun on you," admitted the cowboy. "I wasn't wantin' you to squeeze trigger before I got started talkin'." His voice went hard. "I could have made plenty trouble for you down in the canyon. I seen you layin' there in the bushes."

King thought it over. "Move out where I can see you," he said.

"Me and you both," bargained Sandy. "Guns back in leather."

"All right," agreed King. He holstered his gun, took another look, saw the cowboy's blurred shape lifted from the sagebrush.

They moved toward each other, cautious, watchful, and King said grimly, "All right. What's on your mind?"

Sandy's face was pale in the violet glow of the fading twilight. "Mebbe I'm loco." His voice was troubled. "I kind of liked the way you come and rode the boss back to the ranch."

"Garson couldn't have made it on foot," King said.

"There's a lot of folks wouldn't have cared a damn."

The bitterness in his voice made King wonder.

"He's your boss," he reminded. "You stood by him back there, would have killed me with your rocks if I hadn't been too quick for you."

"I'm takin' his pay," Sandy said. "So long as I'm on his payroll, I'm on his side."

King nodded. He knew and respected the iron code that held a cowboy's loyalty to the man whose pay he took.

"I ain't takin' no more pay from him," Sandy went on, his voice tight. "Not after what I seen done at Carroll's place today."

King felt suddenly cold. Something terrible had happened to Mary Carroll, something too shocking for even this hardened young cowboy to endure.

He forced himself to speak. "What do you mean?"

Sandy was studying him intently. "There was talk about you back at JC," he said. "Seems like you're that King Malory feller that busted jail."

"That's my name," King admitted.

"They claim you're a rustler."

"Never mind about me," interrupted King. "What's this trouble at the Carroll ranch?"

"Jim Carroll figgers you stole the cows he left back at Mesquite Springs," Sandy told him, his voice hard. "Santeen figgers he's lyin', or in cahoots with you. That's why he's rode old Carroll back to Bar G." The cowboy paused, added significantly, "Garson hates old man Carroll's guts."

"I want to know about the girl," King said, his voice husky.

Sandy's eyes took on the look of blue ice. "I'm wantin' to know if you rustled them cows."

"What's it to you?" King asked.

"I've swore I'm killin' the man who done it!" Sandy told him. "I'm backin' that gal's pa to the limit."

A grin spread over King's face. He said soberly, "You can count me in on that play, Sandy." He thrust out a hand. "Shake. We're riding the same trail."

They gripped hands, and Sandy said in a puzzled voice, "I cain't make out your game a-tall, Malory." His lip lifted in a thin smile. "I been doin' plenty thinkin' about you, and about all I got is you're sure one white man clean down to your boot heels."

"Never mind about me," repeated King. "Tell me about the girl. Is she all right?"

"She was hellbent for town last time I seen her." Sandy grinned. "Sure has plenty nerve, that Carroll gal. You should have seen the way she pulled a gun on Dal Santeen." He shook his head. "Didn't have a chance." He described the scene in the ranchyard. "We rode off with the old man," he continued. "I seen Dal Santeen sneak back, figgered he was up to no good and trailed him. He made a grab for her mare when she rode out of the yard." Sandy's grin widened. "I took a shot at him and his bronc went loco, pitched Santeen on his haid and sure hightailed it away from there. Mary done the same."

King was silent for a long moment. The story had shaken him, also left him enormously relieved. He said, softly, "I knew there was good stuff in you, Sandy. You're the kind of man I want siding me."

The cowboy hesitated, his expression doubtful. "I'm tellin' you now, Malory, that I figger to go straight from this time on."

"Meaning you'll want to know if I'm really a cow thief?" King kept his face grave.

Sandy nodded. "That's right." He scowled. "It's my notion the talk about you is all wrong. Like I said, I ain't figgered out your game, but I'm damn sure it ain't rustlin'."

King studied him. Right now he was in desperate need of a friend, and this man was offering him his friendship, his trust.

He said, his voice quiet, "I'm not a rustler, Sandy. Will you take my word for it?"

"Sure." Sandy grinned, "Mebbe I'm actin' some loco, but I'm layin' my bet you ain't no rustler."

"You won't lose your bet," King assured him. He paused. "Won't Santeen wonder what's become of you?"

The cowboy shook his head, amusement in his eyes. "I told him I thought I seen his bronc down on the slope. He figgers I'm scoutin' round for sign."

King nodded, asked another question. "How come Santeen doesn't know it was your shot that set his bronc to pitching back at the Carroll ranch?"

"That was easy," grinned the cowboy. "I lit a shuck away from there, then headed back to him on the run.

Santeen was hawg-wild, nursin' a broke arm. Made out I'd heard the shot and was wonderin' what was wrong. I fixed up a sling for him, got a JC bronc from the barn and that's the story. Santeen don't suspect nothin'."

"You're sure he doesn't?"

"Yeah." Sandy nodded. "Sure."

"That's fine." King paused. "We've got to get Jim Carroll away from there in a hurry. You know your way around that place and nobody suspects you. That makes you an ace card in the play."

Sandy nodded, his face grim. "I'm listenin'."

"You get going. Tell Santeen you couldn't find track of his horse."

"I savvy."

"Keep your ears open, learn all you can about Carroll."

Sandy nodded. "Sure."

"I'll be around after dark," King continued. "I'll want to get in touch with you."

Sandy considered the problem. "I can meet you in the gully back of the horse corral," he finally decided. He told King how to find the gully. "I'll be watchin' for you," he promised.

"I reckon that's all for now," King said. "All right, Sandy. *Hasta la vista.*"

Sandy said laconically, "You bet." And became a vague, quick-moving shape in the sagebrush.

King found a boulder, sat down, reached again for tobacco sack and papers. His expression was grim. The job he had taken on was not going to be easy. Cole

Garson was a wise old buzzard and he had a tough brood roosting with him. Sandy was indeed an ace card in this desperate game in which the stakes were life or death — winner take all.

CHAPTER
TWELVE

Dark Night

When business was slack Ben Wire had a fondness for the old rawhide rocker under the interlaced branches of the two big chinaberry trees that shaded the long water trough in front of his livery barn. A quid of tobacco stowed comfortably inside a lean and leathery cheek, he could take his ease, drowsily recall more stirring days when he was a hard-riding county sheriff.

There were moments when these reflections put a puzzled look in the still keen blue eyes. He would shake his head, finger the silver star in his shirt pocket. The events that had removed his badge of office from its proper place on his shirt still mystified him. It was Ed Yate's talk that had cost him his re-election. He would still be sheriff if Ed Yate had not yelled so loud about losing too many cows to rustlers. San Lucas cowmen had really believed that Sheriff Ben Wire was asleep on the job.

The liveryman snorted angrily, straightened up in the rawhide rocker. From all the talk he heard, the new sheriff spent most of his time playing poker. He had not caught a rustler in the two years he had been in office. And strangely enough Ed Yate was already boosting the man for re-election. The thing made no sense. There was a bad smell to it.

Ex-Sheriff Ben Wire scowled. Something queer about this King Malory business, the way Ed Yate laid for him at the post office, threw him in jail. Had to drag in a U. S. deputy marshal to do the job. Looked as if Ed figured his pet sheriff was too short on guts to tackle even one lone cow thief. Served Ed right that the young desperado broke jail and got clean away. Malory would still be in jail if a real sheriff had put him there.

Ben Wire's eyes narrowed thoughtfully. The affair had aroused a vague uneasiness in him from the start. Mighty queer the young outlaw should wear the same name of a man who had been hung for a cow thief. The tragedy had been several years before his time, and the story was hazy in his mind. Sam Doan and Pete Walker always looked very solemn when the affair was mentioned. It seemed they used to work for old King Malory, had been with him when he trailed his herd of longhorns up from the Pecos and started the old Circle M ranch, now long since only a faint memory in the San Lucas country. Ed Yate owned the home ranch now. Ed's Flying Y about dominated the San Lucas country and was bigger even than Cole Garson's Bar G ranch. Oddly enough both ranches had been carved from the ruins of old Circle M.

A faint haze of dust lifting above the piñons on the slope beyond the town drew the liveryman's attention. Somebody was taking the shortcut down the old Comanche trail. Coming fast, too, from the looks of that swirling dust.

136

Ben Wire frowned. He knew the trail, its sharp turns — the treacherous shale that could send a horse sliding helplessly over a cliff. The man in the saddle was a reckless fool, or else gripped by some desperate need to get to town in a hurry.

The swirling dust drifted, faded. The rider was crossing the dry wash where the trail cut into the road, and suddenly Ben heard the beat of drumming hoofs. He shook his head. Not coming so fast now. The horse was tired, legs unsteady.

The liveryman got out of his chair, stood there, expectant eyes watching up the street, hat pulled low over badger-gray hair against the sun. A lean, capable-looking man whose seamed, weather-bitten face now showed sudden deep concern.

"Mary Carroll!" he muttered. "Looks like she's in plenty trouble."

The girl saw him, pulled her mare into the yard. She seemed on the verge of a collapse. Ben ran to her. She almost fell into his arms, leaned against him, trembling, inarticulate.

"Ben. Ben." Her voice choked.

He said gently, "Take it easy, Mary. Take it easy," he repeated. He was looking at the sweat-lathered mare, and glimpsing his disapproving expression she drew back, lifted her chin at him.

"Oh, I know you think I'm crazy riding Molly nearly to death, but — but —" She choked up again.

"You're as bad off as the mare," Ben said. "You come and set for a spell, Mary." He tried to edge her toward the chair.

137

She resisted him. "I've no time."

"What's the trouble?" he asked, worried gaze on her. "You look ready to keel over."

"Is — is Ed Yate in town?"

Ben shook his head. "Ed went back to his ranch yesterday."

"Oh, dear!" Mary gestured despairingly. "I don't know what to do."

"You can begin by tellin' me what's wrong," Ben said.

"Garson's foreman came to our place, practically accused Father of being a cow thief, and took him off to Bar G ranch. Santeen had his outfit with him. Father was helpless. I'm terribly frightened."

"Don't make good sense," declared Ben. "Your dad never stole a cow in his life."

"Of course not!" Indignation was steadying her. "Just because Santeen couldn't find our cattle, he claims Father stole them. It's all crazy. How can a man steal his own cattle anyway?"

"Sounds some mixed up," commented Ben. "What for was Santeen lookin' for your dad's cows?"

Mary hesitated. The story of the affair at Mesquite Springs was too fantastic. How could she tell this ex-sheriff that an escaped outlaw had forced Cole Garson to let her father water the JC herd at the springs?

"Why, Mr. Garson didn't like Father using the springs and turning our cattle on his range."

The liveryman eyed her shrewdly. "I reckon I savvy." His tone was grim. "Garson ain't one to give somethin' for nothin'. He figgered to collect plenty, huh?"

138

"It's worse than that," Mary told him. "Mr. Garson hates Father. He made dreadful threats, said he'd run Father out of the country, perhaps get him hung for a cow thief."

"Garson's a doggone schemin' old buzzard," growled Ben. "He never did like Jim Carroll gettin' hold of that west Calabasas range."

Mary nodded. "He claims the survey is all wrong and that the land is really old Circle M range and actually belongs to him."

"Garson's a tough man to buck," Ben worried. "Mebbe would have been good sense for your dad to make a deal with him and get out."

"Father is not that kind of man," Mary told him coldly. "He doesn't scare easily. He's a fighter." She paused, added angrily, "anyway, accepting Garson's offer would have meant ruin."

"I ain't blamin' him none." Ben's face hardened. "I'd feel the same way — tell Garson to go to hell."

"I'm frightened," Mary said. "Father is in terrible danger." She faltered. "I — I was so hoping I'd find Ed Yate in town. He wouldn't let Mr. Garson harm Father. He's always been so nice to us."

"Sure wish I could figger some way to help you." The liveryman's tone was troubled. "If I was still sheriff I'd fork a bronc and head over to Bar G on the jump." He gestured. "The way things are, I'm plumb useless. Garson hates my guts."

Mary thought it over. "I — I'll ask Sam Doan," she decided. "Sam has known Mr. Garson a long time. He might be able to do something."

"Sam and Pete has been out of town last couple of days," Ben told her. "Ain't knowin' for sure if they're back. Sam don't stable his stock here. Has his own barn back of the hotel."

"I'll go over there now." Mary looked at the drooping mare. "You'll take care of Molly for me, Ben?"

"Sure will," he promised. "I'll have Rubio give her a good rubdown."

She hurried up the street to the hotel. The lobby was empty, a plumpish, blond youth at the desk. She had a vague impression she knew him, was unable to recall his name.

"I wanted to see Sam." She had almost run the two blocks from the livery barn, was breathless, flushed.

"Sam isn't in town, Miss Carroll." The blond clerk was using his best smile. "You don't remember me, I think."

His name came to her. "Oh, yes, I do. You're Willie Logan." She made herself smile back at him.

"I'm clerking here full-time now," Willie Logan told her importantly. "I can fix you up with a nice room, Miss Carroll." He inked a pen, held it out.

She could only look at him, her smile a frozen grimace now.

The pen dropped from Willie's fingers. He said in a startled voice, "You — you're crying!" He was suddenly pale. "Miss Carroll, what's wrong?"

"I — I don't know what to do. I — I can't find anybody who might be able to help." Mary drew a handkerchief from the hip pocket of her jeans, dabbed at her eyes.

140

Willie Logan's brief experience as hotel clerk had not prepared him to cope with a weeping lady patron. He rumpled thick wavy hair agitatedly.

"Gosh, Miss Carroll! I — I'm sure awful sorry. Gosh, wish Sam and Pete were here!" His look went to the door, fastened with relief on the man entering the lobby. "Hey, there, Mr. Lestang! Come quick! Miss Carroll — she — she's feeling bad."

Mary tensed as she heard the name. *Lestang!* The saloon man. She recalled Cole Garson's words at Mesquite Springs. *I can give you a note to Vince Lestang. He owes me for a bunch of steers.*

Her spirits started a quick climb from zero. Lestang could intercede with Garson. The two men were business friends. Lestang was important in San Lucas, rich and powerful, a man Garson would want to please. She did not like him, but any tool was welcome if it meant saving her father's life. She must manage to persuade him.

Instinctively she knew it was feminine charm she must use to gain this man's interest, his help. She turned as he came up to the desk, concern on his darkly handsome face.

"Oh, Mr. Lestang, I'm so worried, frightened!" Her face lifted in an appealing look at him. "I'm so dreadfully in need of help."

He said sympathetically, "I saw you running up the street, Miss Carroll. I thought you looked upset and hurried over to see if I could be of assistance." He smiled, touched his waxed mustache, eyes bold, appraising. "Please do call on me. Glad to help."

141

She put warmth into her eyes, a tremulous smile on her lips. "That's nice of you, Mr. Lestang."

He lifted a deprecatory hand. "Not at all, Miss Carroll. My pleasure and privilege to have an opportunity to serve you." He smiled reproachfully. "I have sometimes thought you would never give me a chance to know you better."

"Why, Mr. Lestang!" For a moment Mary was genuinely embarrassed. She colored, and was suddenly aware that his smile did not reach his eyes. There was no warmth there, only thinly veiled curiosity. She plunged on, "I — I never dreamed you cared to know me better. You are so important!"

Her confusion seemed to please him. "Not so important that I haven't time for a pretty girl, Miss Carroll." His voice deepened. "Now, tell me in what way I can be of help."

He listened, attentive, his face without expression while she briefly told him the same story she had given Ben Wire. As before she left out King Malory's part in the affair at Mesquite Springs, made no mention of Dal Santeen's attempt on her. The telling brought the tremble back to her legs. Willie Logan hastily pushed a chair to her.

"Gosh, Miss Carroll." Willie's face was pale. "Don't blame you for feeling scared." He tried to put comfort in his voice. "I reckon Mr. Lestang can do something mighty quick about it." He looked at the saloon man anxiously.

An odd glint came and went in Lestang's eyes. He said smoothly, "We'll start immediately for Bar G, Miss

142

Carroll. It's hard to believe the situation is as serious as you think, but I quite understand your anxiety." He paused, studied her intently. "You look very tired. I suggest you run over to the Home Café for a cup of hot coffee. I'll be waiting for you at the livery barn."

"They've got mighty good stew all ready to serve," observed Willie Logan. "It's a long ride to Bar G, Miss Carroll. You'll feel better with some hot stew in you."

"Good idea, Willie," smilingly approved Lestang. "All right, Miss Carroll." He hurried her to the door, down the porch steps and across the street to the café.

"I'll pick you up in fifteen minutes," he promised. "You won't need to come to the barn."

The evening shadows were crawling as they drove out of town in his easy-riding buckboard. The team, matched bays, traveled fast.

"Morgans," Vince complacently told the girl by his side. "Best trotting horses in the world."

Mary said nothing. Disturbing thoughts were in her mind. She was recalling something Sam Doan had said to her father. *Lestang is so crooked a snake would break its back followin' his trail. Ain't trustin' that smooth-talkin' hombre as far as I can throw a bull.*

She wondered miserably if she had made a mistake putting her trust in this man. His friendship with Cole Garson was no recommendation. Quite the reverse. Sam Doan was a shrewd judge of men. It was entirely possible that Vince Lestang was even more dangerous than Garson.

She lay back against the cushion, closed her eyes, and tried to down the panic rising in her. It was no use. She knew she was afraid — dreadfully afraid.

She heard Lestang's voice. "Sleepy?"

She seized on the chance his question offered to excuse her silence. She felt too ill to attempt conversation.

"Yes, sleepy. Hope you don't mind. I'm so tired."

"Go ahead. Take a nap." His arm slipped behind her. "Poor kid."

Mary's spine cringed under his touch. She was petrified, hardly dared to breath. She wanted to push his arm away, but feared to arouse his resentment.

The last of the twilight faded. Stars sprang out. She sat very still in the fast-moving buckboard, and prayed for strength to face whatever peril the dark night might bring.

CHAPTER
THIRTEEN

In the Face of Danger

The starlight was almost too bright for King. He drew himself over the ledge and crouched close to the long feed shed that extended from the barn to the horse corral. Behind him was the bluff he had just climbed from the blind gully where he had left the buckskin.

Satisfied that he had not been seen, he edged around the low building for a look across the ranchyard. He heard a distrustful snort from the horse corral, a sudden trample of hoofs. He remained motionless, hugged the deeper shadows of the high fence. The commotion might draw attention.

A man emerged from the stable. He carried a lighted lantern. He stood for a moment gazing over at the horse corral, then moved on down the yard toward the bunk-house.

King's gaze followed him until he disappeared inside. Lamplight glowed from the windows there, and some hundred yards beyond he could see the ranch house lights winking through the trees.

The place seemed peaceful enough. No sounds to indicate anything unusual. Only the restless stamp of the horses in the corral, the low murmur of voices from the bunkhouse. It was plain that Bar G was not expecting trouble.

His taut nerves relaxed. He was reluctant to believe Sandy guilty of treachery. Something unforeseen must have prevented the cowboy from keeping the rendezvous in the gully. Or else Sandy was in serious trouble. It was quite possible that Santeen had become suspicious.

A man came out of the bunkhouse. Light flowing from the open door showed a guitar in his hands. He sat on the step, plucked a few notes from the guitar, and began to sing in a high, nasal voice.

By the time he had reached the second mournful verse, King was in the cottonwoods behind the bunkhouse. He crept close to the window and took a cautious look inside.

Five men sat at a table engrossed in a poker game. A sixth man sprawled on a bunk, reading a dog-eared mail order catalogue. Another man sat astride a wooden bench mending a bridle. He lifted his head, took up the song in a husky bass.

Oh, bury me deep on the lone prairie —

King ducked away, moved on soundless feet toward the ranch house. His brief glance had told him that Sandy was not in the bunkhouse. Nor had he recognized Cisco among them.

His anxiety mounted. Losing Sandy was losing his ace card in this desperate game with its high stakes of life or death. He was on unfamiliar ground, hardly knew where to look for Jim Carroll.

He reached the high hedge that completely encircled the ranch house grounds. The clatter of pans and dishes drifted to him as he crouched there.

King slid along the hedge to the white picket gate, opened it cautiously for fear of a squeaky hinge. He slipped through and, warned in time by the slam of a screen door, flattened behind a squat adobe building that he guessed was the dairy house.

He took a stealthy look, saw the cook framed in the light from the kitchen door — a small skinny man with an untidy drooping mustache, and an apron tied around his middle.

Apparently, it was the endless song from the bunk-house that had drawn the cook out to the back porch. He stood there listening critically, fingers busy twisting a cigarette. He joined softly in the refrain, put a match to the cigarette, and slammed back into his kitchen.

King, wasting no time, slipped quickly across the open space into the shadow of the trees on the far side of the house. His purpose now was to get into the little back garden overlooked by the windows of Cole Garson's luxurious ranch office.

He found the gate, opened it carefully, saw the bright light of the windows. The curtains had not been drawn.

He crept close, stood behind a bush and got his first look into the room. His heart sank. Sandy was there, his holster empty, his hands tied behind his back. Standing behind him was Cisco and his fellow guard, guns in their hands, and slumped dejectedly in the same chair King had occupied earlier that day was Jim Carroll.

Cole Garson sat opposite him, huddled back in his huge chair, his face an expressionless mask, and standing near him, his back to the windows, was the tall, lean shape of Dal Santeen.

King crawled closer, bent low under one of the open windows. He heard Garson's thin, querulous voice.

"Too late now to dicker, Carroll. We might have done business last week." His tone grew venomous. "You threw in with an outlaw, a rustler, planned to steal my water, my range. You put my life in jeopardy."

Carroll said hoarsely, "A damn lie!"

"You threw in with a cow thief," Garson continued implacably. "I've got you red-handed, Jim Carroll. You've been fooling honest cattlemen a long time. The Association won't need to look further for this mysterious rustler chief. You're him, Carroll."

"It's a lie," repeated the JC man. He gestured despairingly. "I never stole a cow in all my born days."

Garson's eyes glittered. "You and this King Malory have been in cahoots a long time," he accused. "Malory knows his way around this country too well to be a stranger. You tell him the ranches to raid and he does the actual stealing. You can't deny it, Carroll. You and Malory boss this rustler gang. I've got you, and I'll get him, and that will put an end to cow stealing in the San Lucas country."

"Give me a chance to talk to Ed Yate," begged the distraught rancher. "Ed will say you're crazy."

Something like a grimace broke the expressionless mask of Garson's face. He said softly, "You're wrong, Carroll. You won't get any help from Ed Yate, even if he *is* the president of the Stockmen's Association."

"My girl," muttered Carroll. "She — she'll —" His voice choked.

Garson picked up a paper from his desk, glanced at it, looked at Carroll. "I'm sorry for the girl," he said primly. "You can help her out of a bad fix if you'll sign this piece of paper, Carroll."

"What is it?" asked Mary's father.

"A quit claim deed to your ranch." Garson pursed his lips. "Sign it, Carroll, and I'll promise to hand one thousand dollars over to your girl. Enough for her to get away to some new town."

"You lowdown snake!" frothed Carroll.

"Suit yourself." Garson shrugged. "I'll get the ranch anyway. It saves me some trouble if you sign, and your girl gets a thousand. She's going to be in a bad fix if you don't sign."

Carroll hesitated, a stricken look on his haggard face. He said in a husky whisper, "I'll sign."

Garson pushed the paper forward, handed him a pen. Carroll signed. His hand was trembling and the pen made loud scratching sounds in that momentary hush.

Garson said curtly, "You sign, too, as witness, Dal."

The foreman bent over the paper, scrawled hastily.

King's fingers were hard on the gun butt as he crouched there. He could kill Santeen and the two guards, kill Garson. He had the advantage of surprise.

Four quick shots and the office would be a shambles. He was fast, and he did not miss his shots. Four men would die in as many seconds.

Common sense warned him against such folly. The shots would bring the Bar G men on the run. Escape would be impossible. He must think of some other solution to the grim problem confronting him.

Carroll was speaking, his voice hopeless. "You're holding me for the sheriff?"

"He'll be over from Deming in a day or two," Garson replied. "I'll send the word to him."

"You could turn me over to Ed Yate," suggested Carroll.

Garson shook his head. "I don't think much of the San Lucas jail. King Malory broke out of there too easy, and you've too many friends in that town." He turned his head in a look at the Bar G foreman. "I'm leaving it to you to keep Carroll safe for the sheriff, Dal. If he attempts an escape, you'll know what to do." There was deadly emphasis in his thin voice. "You understand?"

The Bar G foreman nodded, said laconically, "I savvy."

King felt suddenly cold. He understood, too. Jim Carroll was to be murdered. The sheriff would be told the prisoner had been killed while attempting to escape.

He heard Santeen's rasping voice, "What do you figger to do with Sandy Wells?" He glared at the cowboy. "If Cisco hadn't been watchin' close, the skunk would have got Carroll away from here."

150

Garson's unwinking look fastened on Sandy. "You know what happens to men who try to double-cross me, boy."

Sandy said in a low, tight voice, "You damn old buzzard. To hell with you!"

Garson's hand lifted in a gesture of dismissal. "I'm leaving Sandy to you, Dal. You know what to do."

Sandy stared at the foreman, his blue eyes hard, defiant. "I sure wish my bullet had got you 'stead of your bronc," he said bitterly.

Santeen's face reddened with anger as he took a quick step and slapped the cowboy's face. "So it was you flung that bullet, huh?" Rage choked his voice.

Garson's hand lifted again. "Listen," he interrupted.

There was a silence. King heard the light rattle of buckboard wheels, the unmistakable hoof thuds of a fast moving team.

Garson said, "See who's coming, Dal. Might be Vince." He looked thoughtfully at Carroll and Sandy. "Whoever it is, don't get back too quick. Give Cisco time to get these men away. I don't want 'em seen."

The foreman nodded and hurried from the room. King heard the slam of the front door. The visitor must be Vince Lestang, the saloon man who dealt in land and cattle. According to Sam Doan he had recently acquired the Calabasas range. It seemed logical to believe that Lestang was the frequent visitor described by Manuel Cota. *One who comes is very grand and wears a black mustache with wax on it.*

Anxious as he was to glimpse the man and verify his identity, King knew the matter must wait. Only immediate action now could save Carroll and Sandy. He had perhaps five minutes before Santeen returned with this late caller who might be Vince Lestang.

He crept steathily around the corner, and came to the side door. It was open, but there still remained the screen door. He touched it gently, inched it open, got a foot against it ready for a swift plunge into the room.

Garson was speaking. "Tie Carroll's hands," he said to Cisco.

The man holstered his gun, drew a short length of cord from a pocket and motioned for the rancher to get out of the chair. The rancher obeyed, stood by Sandy, the other guard watchful, gun ready. Like the others, his back was turned to the patio door. Garson gave the prisoners an indifferent glance, picked up the grant deed, and began to crease it into folds.

It was now or never. King slipped into the room, silent as a swift-moving panther, jabbed his gun against the guard's spine. The man let out a stifled gasp, went rigid and in an instant King's lightning reach had snatched the gun from his fear-paralyzed fingers.

The whisper of sound behind him drew Cisco's attention. He swung around, stared into the menacing barrel of the second gun. His face suddenly ashen, he dropped the cord, lifted his hands.

King hardly more than glanced at Garson. He had learned earlier in the day that the man was a physical coward. He stepped back, guns covering the two horrified Bar G men; and Carroll, coming out of his apathy, snatched up the cord and swiftly tied Cisco's

152

wrists behind his back. He jerked the man's gun from its holster, leveled it at Garson now huddled terror-stricken in his huge chair, the deed clutched in his hand.

King shook his head. "Never mind Garson," he said. "Get Sandy loose."

Carroll pushed the gun into his own holster, drew a clasp knife from his pocket and cut the knots. Sandy snatched up the cord, gave King a dancing-eyed look and went to work tying up the second guard.

Perhaps a minute had passed. King moved swiftly to Garson, snatched the deed from his fingers, thrust it into a pocket and jerked Garson to his feet. He dipped the pen in ink, held it out, motioned at a sheet of blank paper. "Write what I say!"

Garson was shaking. He smelled death very close. He bent over the sheet of paper, wrote the few words King dictated:

Dal, you and Vince wait here. I'll be back in a few minutes.

King nodded satisfaction, leaned the note against the inkwell, motioned Garson to precede him to the side door. Sandy had a gun in his hand now. He gave Cisco a prod in the ribs.

"Get movin,' feller." His low voice was exultant.

Garson and the two guards trooped out, the three armed men close at their backs. They reached the patio gate.

King said in a harsh whisper, "We're going to the barn. If one of you wants to die quick, just start something."

"Me, I ain't startin' nothin'," muttered Cisco.

King tapped Garson with the barrel of his gun. "Understand, Garson? If anybody sees us it's just the boss and some of the boys headed for the barn. One false move and I'll kill you."

Garson nodded that he understood, and they passed into the kitchen yard. King was thankful to hear sounds from the kitchen that told him the cook was still busy with his pots and pans.

He herded the prisoners into the darkness behind the dairy house, and told Sandy to take a look in the yard.

The cowboy was back in a few seconds, reported that Santeen and the visitor had gone into the house. "It's Lestang all right," he said. "Had a feller with him. Couldn't see him good. Too dark under the trees. The choreman's unhookin' the team," he added. "He'll head for the barn with 'em."

King thought it over, his expression worried. "You know your way around this place," he said. "Think fast, Sandy. We've got to get away from here in a hurry."

The bunkhouse balladist was singing *La Paloma* and getting in a lot of fancy notes from his guitar. King hoped he would keep it up. Music from the bunkhouse would make Santeen think that all was well outside. He would wait a reasonable time for Garson to reappear before suspecting anything wrong.

Sandy said softly, "There's a hole someplace here in the hedge. We can take these skunks back of the bunk-house on the other side of the cottonwoods, work round the corral, and get into the barn through the rear door."

They found the gap. Sandy went first, waited on the other side of the hedge, his gun ready, while King and Jim Carroll prodded the prisoners through.

Starlight showed the vague outlines of a building that King had not noticed before because of the trees. He asked Sandy about it.

"Used to be the granary," Sandy told him. "Don't use it any more since the big one was built up by the barn."

"Got a door?" King asked.

"Sure," Sandy assured him, quick to get the drift of the questions. "A key in the door, too, last time I was over there, and no windows a man can crawl through. Only six inch slits for air and 'dobe walls a couple of feet thick."

Garson opened his mouth as if about to protest. King waggled his gun at him. "Not a whisper," he warned. "Get moving." He gestured at the squat adobe. "Over there."

They moved toward the adobe. Cisco pretended to stumble, straightened up with a gasp as Sandy jabbed his gun into him.

"I'll knock you cold if you try that trick again," warned the cowboy. "I'll bust your head wide open."

They reached the door. King saw with satisfaction that it was a stout affair strapped with iron. He

155

motioned for the prisoners to go inside. He followed, grasped Garson's arm, held him tight.

"Find something to tie him up, Sandy," he said. "You stand watch outside, Mr. Carroll."

"Seen some old ropes layin' over in a corner last time I was in here," Sandy said. He groped around in the darkness, returned with several odd lengths of rope. King stepped back, watching while the cowboy jerked Garson's arms back and tied his wrists.

"Down on your bellies, the three of you," ordered King.

The prisoners obeyed, Cisco cursing under his breath. Sandy tapped him on the head. "Shut your mouth. I'm sure drawin' your knots tight for that."

He worked swiftly, slipped a running noose around Garson's neck and knotted the other end around Cisco's ankles. He treated the other two in the same fashion.

"Reckon that'll hold you good," he said contentedly. "Start rollin' and you'll choke each other to death. Need somethin' to tie up their mouths," he added.

"Use their bandannas," King said.

Sandy bent over Garson. "He ain't got one." He snatched his own bandanna, knotted it securely over Garson's mouth. "You ain't killin' me this trip, you old buzzard," he gibed.

King, anxious to get away, helped with the gags on the other pair. Luck had ridden with them so far, but it would not be long now before Dal Santeen would begin to wonder what was keeping his boss.

The big key was rusty. King had some trouble turning it in the padlock.

"Take an ax to bust that door down," Sandy commented. "Where do we go from here?"

"To the barn." King hurled the key into the brush. "You and Carroll need horses."

With Sandy in the lead, they hurried away, careful to hug the shadowed fence. King blessed the singing cowboy and his guitar as they stealthily passed the bunkhouse. Not much chance sharp ears would pick up betraying sounds with all that noise going on.

They reached the rear door of the barn. A light burned dimly inside and they could hear the choreman stripping the harness from the buckboard team.

Sandy took a cautious look inside, beckoned to the others, "Quick! He's in the stall and cain't see us."

The choreman backed from the stall, his arms loaded with harness. He heard the rustle of straw under swift-moving feet, turned to look. The harness slid from his arms. He stood there, his fat, unshaved face a pasty green in the lantern light.

Sandy asked softly, "Want for me to knock you in the head, or will you be a good doggie?"

The man said nothing, just nodded his head.

"So scared he cain't speak," chuckled the cowboy. He snatched a coil of rope from a peg, holstered his gun. "Get down on your face, Fat."

The choreman's weak knees were already wobbling. He almost fell in his haste to obey. King took the rope from Sandy.

157

"You and Carroll throw on saddles," he said. "I'll do this job."

Jim Carroll had already spotted his baldy horse. He dragged the saddle from the peg, went to work. Sandy hurried to a roan horse several stalls down, reached for his saddle.

Their horses were ready by the time King had finished tying and gagging the choreman. In a moment they had the helpless man dumped into a manger. Sandy picked up the lantern, blew out the lights and tossed the lantern into another manger.

They were outside again with the horses. Sandy looked at the flush over the eastern hills.

"Moon comin'," he muttered. "Let's get away from here before our luck breaks."

"Can you get down to the gully with the horses," King asked.

The cowboy nodded, "Sure." He swung into his saddle. Jim Carroll climbed into his. He gave King an odd look. "I'm taking it back, Malory. You wouldn't be doing this if you had stole my cows."

King said briefly, "Get moving. I'll be waiting in the gully."

He watched until they disappeared, swung over the ledge and worked his way cautiously down the steep bluff.

He was in his saddle when the others rode out of a narrow gap. The moon shot over the mountains and light touched his grimly exultant face. He drew the quit claim deed from his pocket. "You'll want to tear it up, Jim," he said.

Jim Carroll said simply, "You bet!" He reached for the folded document, tore it to shreds and tossed the pieces to the night wind.

King grinned, swung his horse into the down trail.

Jim and Sandy followed, wordless, their faces sober, a curious awe in their eyes. They had never known a man like this laconic King Malory who had risked his own life to save theirs.

Sandy glanced at the big-framed ranchman riding by his side. "I'd go to hell and back with him any time," he said fervently. "He's my boss from now on."

Jim Carroll nodded gravely. He was thinking of Mary. His heart was too full for words.

CHAPTER
FOURTEEN

Pattern for Murder

Vince Lestang said, "Almost there." he touched the Morgans lightly with his whip and their stride lengthened. The buckboard careened as they whirled down the slope. The road ran straight here, and Mary could see the ranch house lights directly ahead.

It was plain that Vince Lestang was familiar with this road. He must have traveled it many times, or he would not have dared such speed on a night so dark.

She took a cautious look at him. His profile might have been chiseled from stone. The veneer of geniality was gone. His expression frightened her.

He had long since withdrawn his arm, apparently not liking her unyielding stiffness, and for miles there had been hardly a word from him. She had pretended to sleep, was really wide awake and trying to find a glimmer of hope in the dark confusion of her thoughts.

The ranch house lights were close now, winked through the trees as the bay team whirled the buck-board up the avenue. Lestang had not spared these fine horses. They were sweating and blowing when he drew them to a halt in front of a high, white picket gate. Mary guessed it was his way to use things hard, get all he could out of them. Horses or men or women were only conveniences to him, a means to an end. The thought drew a shiver from her. She wished miserably that she had remembered Sam Doan's shrewd opinion of the man in time to keep her from asking his help. Her folly was going to make things more difficult for her father. She had been so desperate. No time to think, or common sense would have warned her that any friend of Cole Garson was dangerous.

Somebody was strumming a guitar, the melody thin and sharp in the stillness of the vast yard. A door slammed and a man's tall shape appeared on the porch, moved quickly down the walk.

Mary felt her flesh prickle. Dal Santeen — surprise, and something more ugly in his eyes as he pushed through the picket gate — recognized her.

Another man hurried up from the barn, fat, bow-legged and smelling of stable and sweat. He stood by the team while Lestang leisurely climbed out between the wheels.

Santeen said, avid gaze on the girl. "Wasn't lookin' for you tonight, Vince." Elation put a purr in his voice. "See you fetched Mary Carroll along with you." His grin widened on her. "Mighty nice of you to drop in, Mary."

His right arm was in a sling, she observed with satisfaction. She wondered if he had learned that it was Sandy Wells who had caused the accident, and saved her from his pawing hands. All to no purpose now, thanks to her own stupidity. Here she was, and there was Santeen, grinning at her. The one bright spot was

161

his obviously broken arm. Too bad the fall had failed to break his neck.

Lestang was speaking. "We're staying overnight, Dal." He helped Mary down from the buckboard. Her knees felt shaky.

"Sure you're staying," assented the foreman. He spoke to the choreman, told him to unhook the team. "Reckon your pa'll be some surprised to see you," he went on to Mary. "He's in the house now havin' a talk with the boss."

The malicious amusement on his face frightened her. She tried to draw comfort from the thought that at least her father was still alive.

She forced herself to answer the man. "It was kind of Mr. Lestang to bring me. I was telling him about the trouble, and he offered to help."

The attempt to indicate that Lestang was on her side drew a skeptical guffaw from Santeen. Lestang made no comment. His hand was on her arm, pushing her through the gate. The press of his fingers was not friendly and hurt her. She suppressed a hysterical impulse to turn on him and claw his face.

Santeen led the way and they followed him into the hall to the door of the ranch office. The foreman pushed the door open, halted abruptly, muttered an astonished exclamation, strode quickly to the big table desk.

Lestang's hand dropped from her arm. He motioned to a chair.

"Sit down."

She was glad to sit down and hide the fact that she was trembling. The empty room had given her a shock. Santeen had said her father was having a talk with Garson. It was plain the empty room had startled the foreman.

She watched him standing there, frowning at a piece of paper he snatched from the desk. He suddenly gave Lestang a grin, tossed the piece of paper down.

"Boss says he had to go somewhere for a few minutes. Wants for us to wait."

Lestang nodded, sank into a chair. "A drink would go down good after that drive," he said languidly.

"Sure!" Santeen went to an ornate chest in a corner of the room, jerked open a drawer. "What you want, Vince. Whisky, brandy, wine?"

"Whisky," Lestang answered.

Santeen selected a bottle, placed it on the table. "You open it, Vince. Cain't handle it with only one hand to use. I'll rustle up glasses."

Lestang got out of the chair, drew the cork. The foreman brought glasses, fine crystal, Mary noticed. It was her first visit to Cole Garson's ranch. The luxurious office was a fascinating revelation of the man. It was obvious he spared no expense on his personal comforts.

Lestang filled a glass, looked inquiringly at her. She shook her head. It was a time to keep her wits about her.

He smiled, as if reading her thoughts, motioned for Santeen to take the glass. The two men drank, refilled their glasses and drank again.

Lestang returned to his chair, selected a cigar from an expensive-looking case. He lit the cigar, smoked in silence. Santeen moved restlessly about the long room, fingers twisting a cigarette. His face wore a puzzled look.

"Sure is taking plenty time," he muttered.

Lestang removed his cigar. "You could take a look around," he suggested.

Santeen was not listening. He was staring at the hangings that draped the windows overlooking the small garden.

He said, his voice uneasy, "Should be cords on them curtains, tyin' 'em back. Sure ain't there now." He went to the whisky bottle, filled his glass. He drank slowly, puzzled gaze on the hangings, slammed the glass down, and suddenly hurried from the room.

Mary sat very still, conscious of Lestang's watchful eyes. There was mystery in the air, a crisis imminent. Something had happened. She must be ready for anything, keep down her rising panic.

She could hear Santeen out in the hall. He was shouting, running. He dashed into the room, alarm and anger on his face.

"The boss ain't anywhere around!" he told Lestang furiously. "Looks like hell's bust loose here."

Lestang was on his feet now. He moved close to the girl as if afraid she would run from the room. Feet clattered up the hall and a scrawny man with a white apron poked a startled face through the door.

"Where's the boss?" yelled Santeen.

The cook shook his head. "Ain't seen him since supper," he stuttered.

Santeen swore, pushed him aside, ran down the hall. They heard the slam of the kitchen door. He was yelling as he ran.

The cook gave Mary a frightened, wondering look, then faded from view. Lestang waited, frowning gaze on her. She felt he was wondering what he could do with her.

The outside night was suddenly alive with yelling men now. The search was on. Mary listened. Her heart was beating too fast. She must keep cool. The excitement could mean only one thing. Her father had managed to escape. It seemed impossible, but what else could explain Santeen's rage and the frantic search for Garson.

A sudden thought took her breath. Sandy Wells! Sandy had done it, got her father away. It seemed the only answer, unless, and she held her breath again — unless it was King Malory.

She knew that Lestang was eying her strangely. The sudden color in her cheeks, her shining eyes, puzzled him. She lifted her gaze to him, met his look squarely.

"You seem upset, Mr. Lestang." The answering glint of annoyance in his eyes pleased her. "You look really worried." There was a hint of malice in the faint smile that curved her lips.

He went abruptly to the whisky bottle, filled and drained his glass, faced her again, his urbane smile back.

"Excitement becomes you, Miss Carroll, or may I call you Mary, now that we are to be such close friends?"

She froze under the roving boldness of his predatory eyes.

He purred on, "You are too beautiful for those jeans. We must get you out of them, dress that lovely body the way it should be dressed."

Two men ran into the little garden, quick-moving shapes in the lifting moonlight. They went pounding away. A gate slammed behind them.

Mary heard Santeen's voice. He was suddenly in the room again. He was breathing hard, a gun in lowered hand.

"Cain't locate the boss no place," he told Lestang. "Cisco and Red gone, too." He shook his head angrily. "Looks like Carroll and Sandy got away from us, Vince. Two broncs gone from the barn and Fat layin' hawg-tied in a manger. They must have jumped him when he was stripping the harness off your team. Harness layin' there in the straw where he dropped it."

Black rage stared from Vince Lestang's eyes, and Santeen said hurriedly, almost defensively, "Ain't *my* fault. I wasn't gone from here ten minutes. Just don't savvy a-tall what happened. Cisco and Red was watchin' things and Sandy was tied up. Beats me how come him and Carroll got away."

"Garson is around some place close," almost snarled the saloon man. "They didn't carry him off, and Cisco and Red." He paused. "Only two horses gone from the barn, you said?"

Santeen nodded, his face sullen. "Carroll's baldy horse. Sandy took his roan. He owns that bronc. Cain't claim he's a horse thief."

They looked at Mary. Her eyes were bright, defiant, gave no hint of the fear in her. Her father had escaped, but they had her in his stead. Her own fault for allowing desperate anxiety to muddle her wits.

She said, her voice surprisingly steady, "You might as well take me back to town, Mr. Lestang. No use for me to stay now that my father has gone."

It was apparent that her coolness staggered him. He stared at her, speechless. And it was Dal Santeen who answered her.

"I reckon not, Mary." His smile was ugly and the desire hot in his eyes sent a wave of terror through her. "I'm thinkin' your pa will head back this way when he learns you're visitin' Bar G."

Loud yells suddenly broke the brief hush outside. The two men tensed, stood listening. The cook came clattering up the hall, burst into the room, apron balled up in his fist. "They found the boss in the old grain shed." A grin contorted his leathery face. "Him and Cisco and Red, tied up and gags in their jaws."

Booted feet pounded up the hall, and Mary, huddled in the chair, suddenly felt the impact of Cole Garson's eyes as he paused in the door. Dust and cobwebs clung to his black clothes and there was a cut on his lip. One of the men had a supporting arm under his elbow.

Garson shook it off, walked stiffly to his big chair, sank down, head against the cushioned back. He said irritably in his piping voice, "Get out. All of you, except Cisco and Red."

The cowboys, clustered in the doorway, tiptoed back down the hall. Garson's look returned to Mary. "How did she get here?" he asked.

She heard her own voice answering. "Mr. Lestang and I came to see about my father."

Garson's look questioned the saloon man. Lestang shook his head.

"I ran into her in town," he said. "It seemed best to get her away from there before she had a chance to talk."

Mary's eyes blazed at him. "I was a silly fool to trust you."

He ignored her. "I thought something was doing from the way she nearly killed her mare getting to town," he continued. "So I followed her into the hotel. Let her think I was bringing her here to talk you into turning Carroll loose."

Garson nodded, seemed to remember something, looked anxiously at the desk. He scowled, touched his sore lip.

"They took the deed I got Carroll to sign," he grumbled. He brushed at a cobweb on his sleeve, and again Mary felt the impact of his unwinking coal-dust eyes.

Dal Santeen was glowering at the two cowboys, silent, nervous. Like Garson they were dusty and disheveled.

"How come you let a maverick like Sandy Wells pull this play off, and him tied up?" he asked bitterly.

Garson spoke for them, his voice thin as a razor's edge. "The answer is King Malory," he told the startled foreman.

Cisco found his voice. "That feller's hell on wheels. Fastest play I ever seen pulled off." There was grudging admiration in his husky voice, an unmistakable awe.

Garson nodded agreement. The baffled look on Santeen's face seemed to amuse him. Mary wondered at the man's self-control. He had been badly used, bound and gagged, left helpless in a dirty grain shed. His calmness was satanic, and increased her dread of him. He was gloating over her, already planning how to make use of her.

Vince Lestang put her thoughts into words. "She's valuable, Cole," he said.

Again Garson nodded. "King Malory's sweet on her." He made the statement placidly. "He'll be back this way."

Mary's breath quickened. He was right. King Malory would return — and to his death. She felt she could not bear it.

Garson went on talking. "Anybody know you brought the girl here?" he asked Lestang. "Was Sam Doan in the hotel?"

Lestang shook his head. "Only the kid he sometimes gets to clerk at the desk. He knows."

"Nobody else?" persisted Garson. "It's important, Vince."

"Ben Wire knows she drove off with me," answered the saloon man. "He could make a guess."

Garson brushed at another cobweb, his expression thoughtful. "It should be simple," he muttered, as if thinking aloud. He straightened up, his voice piping, shrill.

"Cisco, you and Red throw on saddles and head for town. Get there in a hurry." He paused, looked at Lestang. "You think this kid clerk will still be on the job?"

"He'll be there," the saloon man assured him. He seemed to guess the reason of the question, showed his teeth in a wolfish grin. "He'll likely be asleep in his desk chair, but he'll be there."

"All the better." Garson nodded. "All right, Cisco. If you find him asleep, make sure he never wakes up. If he's awake, put him to sleep for good. Understand?"

"I savvy, boss." Cisco's face showed no emotion. Apparently, murder was nothing new to him.

"I want you to give Ben Wire the same dose of sleeping powder," smiled his boss.

"Got plenty of the same here," the man said callously. He patted the gun in his holster, went quickly from the room, his fellow killer at his heels.

Mary's heart shriveled. They were going to murder young Willie Logan and Ben Wire, and for only one reason. They were the only two people in San Lucas who knew she had accompanied Vince Lestang to the Bar G ranch. She wanted to scream, could only stare in her horror.

Garson was speaking again. "Dal, send a man to the Carroll place. There's a chance Malory and the girl's father will show up there looking for her. They won't pick up her trail in San Lucas, not if Cisco and Red get there first and do a good job. They're sure to make for the ranch and I want them to find this note."

He scribbled rapidly on a sheet of paper, tossed it at the foreman.

Santeen read the message, grinned. "I reckon that's bait for 'em." He hurried away.

There was a long silence, the two men looking at the girl. She made an effort, lifted her chin.

"You've got to let me go." Her voice seemed a long way off.

"We don't have any women in this house," Garson said. "Have a nice room, though, where you can be comfortable." His hand went to a cord. A bell jangled somewhere.

Footsteps hurried up the hall. The cook poked an inquiring face inside the door.

"Take Miss Carroll to the Spanish room," Garson told him. He thought a moment. "You can fix her up a pot of coffee and food if she wants it." His hand lifted. "All right, Miss Carroll. Rincon will fix you up."

Mary got out of her chair, walked dazedly to the door. Her brain felt numb at that moment. Only one thing made coherence in her mind. King Malory would come. They would kill him. Or would they? King Malory was like no man she had ever known. These callous men might have an unpleasant surprise when King Malory came back looking for her.

Her step lightened as she followed Rincon along the hall.

CHAPTER
FIFTEEN

Gunfire

Moonlight lay on the trail where it broke through the dense junipers, touched Sam Doan as he halted his horse. The worry that had been with him for some two days now had grooved deeper the lines in his face.

He felt in a pocket for the stub of tobacco, filled his cheek with a sizeable quid, chewed thoughtfully, his gaze on the town below.

The lights down there were few at this late hour, now after midnight. It was easy to pick them out, the two big swing lanterns in Ben Wire's livery yard, welcome beacons to many a road-weary freighter, the softer glow in front of Lestang's Palace, the night lamp in Joe Slocum's store. Joe always kept a light going in the post office for the benefit of the town marshal's watchful eyes.

Sam's gaze fastened on the hotel. Lamplight glowed softly from the lobby windows, and from several of the upstairs rooms.

His too solemn face took on a more cheerful look. The signs indicated that Willie Logan had been registering some guests. The hotel was needing business, was still in debt to Ed Yate for the loan. Ed had as good as said he would like a substantial payment. Been nice about it though when Sam told him things were slow. Said for Sam not to worry.

Sam winced as he recalled the incident. It had hurt, Ed's asking him about the loan. Come to think of it, the hotel was Ed's idea. He had said he wanted Sam and Pete to take things more easy, offered to put up the money for the hotel to try to compensate for the injuries caused by the stampede. Sam had signed a note for the money, a mere formality, Ed had assured him, and necessary to keep his accounts straight.

A frown furrowed Sam's brow as he thought it over. Putting his name on a piece of paper had meant nothing to him at the time. If Ed Yate had said outright he wanted Sam to repay the money, the thing would have been plain enough. What worried Sam was the fact that the money was supposed to be compensation, not a loan. He had not dreamed that Ed would ask to have the money back. It seemed that signing that piece of paper had as good as made Ed Yate the real owner of the San Lucas Hotel.

Sam eased his big body in the saddle, reflectively curried his nose with the steel hook. He was not liking the way Ed Yate was acting. He had the odd feeling that Ed was planning to get the hotel away from him, fix things so he and Pete would have to get out of town. Come to think of it, the whole damn thing began to smell. Never had been any real reason why Ed wanted him and Pete off the Flying Y payroll. Losing a hand made no difference to holding down a job as foreman, and Pete could still ride any bronc ever foaled and not pull leather.

"Somethin's awful wrong," Sam gloomily told his fidgety horse. "Looks like plenty trouble stormin' up, old feller."

The horse laid ears back, pawed dust. Sam grinned. "Cravin' to get on home, huh," he chuckled.

The trail pitched sharply, crossed a brush-choked ravine, went up the opposite slope in a series of looping turns. Sam let the horse pick his way, halted again as they topped the ridge. He could see the hotel just below the bluff. The upstairs windows were dark now, but lights still glowed from the lobby. The only sounds that reached him came from the Border Palace, the tinkle of a piano, a woman's laugh, thin and sharp in that stillness.

Willie Logan was going to be surprised. He wouldn't be looking for his boss to show up at two o'clock in the morning. He'd most likely be asleep. He'd be upset for the boss to find him asleep.

Sam grinned indulgently. Willie was a good boy. He'd make a lot smarter hotel man than a wore-out old cowman could ever hope to be. Willie had hotel savvy, knew how to treat folks, give 'em the glad hand.

Something stirred down there where a patch of moonlight silvered the yard back of the hotel. A prowling dog, or a coyote.

Sam stiffened in his saddle. That crawling shape was a man, standing upright now, and the shape behind him was another man. Even as he watched, they disappeared behind the dark bulk of the tankhouse.

He wasted no time, dropped from his saddle and went swiftly down the steep bluff, soft-footed as a stalking mountain lion. No time to follow the winding trail.

He glimpsed the men again, vague blurs that moved stealthily toward the hotel porch, hugging the shadows.

A loose rock gave way under him and he went down the last ten feet of the bluff in a staggering run, managed to land on his feet.

Startled by the noise of his abrupt descent, the prowlers were instantly drifting back to the chaparral. Sam guessed they were making for their horses. He ran to intercept them.

The man in the lead glimpsed him as he slid from the brush into the revealing moonlight. Red fire seemed to streak from his quickly lifted hand and even as the crashing gunshot shattered the night's hush Sam's own gun was spitting flame. The man staggered, fell on his face.

The other man's gun was belching lead now. Sam felt his hat lift from his head. He ducked behind a bush, glimpsed a fast-moving shape on the chaparral's edge. He flung a quick shot, and the shape suddenly stopped moving.

A shout broke the brief hush. Willie Logan's voice. The screen door slammed. He came on the run from the porch. He was carrying a shotgun.

Sam called out, "Hold it, son."

Willie froze to a standstill, and the moonlight showed amazement on his face.

Sam spoke again. "Looks like I got me a couple of sneakin' coyotes." He stood up, moved cautiously to the body sprawled in the yard. One look was sufficient. The man was dead.

An upstairs window slammed open. "What's goin' on down there?" The speaker poked a tousled head out of the window.

"You tell me, mister!" Sam moved across the yard to where the second man lay sprawled under a bush. There was still life in this one. Sam rolled him over, picked up the gun that was too near the outflung hand. A second gun was in its holster. He removed it, straightened up.

"All right, Willie," he called. "Get goin' for Doc Brown on the run."

"You all right, Sam?" Willie's voice was anxious.

"Sure. Get goin', son. I want to keep this feller alive long enough for him to do some talkin'."

Willie dashed away, disappearing around the hotel.

Sam heard the staccato clatter of his feet on the planked walk.

More faces were peering from upstairs windows now, and sounds down the street told Sam that the Border Palace revelers were coming on the run to learn the cause of the shooting. He heard a low voice, saw a crouching shape in the bushes, recognized Ben Wire.

He said, "Come on over, Ben."

The liveryman joined him. He had a gun in each hand. He stared hard at the prostrate man.

"Looks like Cisco," he said.

Sam nodded. " Sure is."

More shapes appeared, drifted in from the street. Sam recognized Ed Yate.

"What's wrong, Sam?" The cattleman came up, gazed wonderingly at the wounded man.

"Ask me somethin' easy," growled Sam.

Ben Wire said softly, "Here's Cliff Burl."

The town marshal shouldered through the little crowd that had gathered on the corner. He was beefy in build and face, and there was suspicion and dislike in the look he gave Sam.

"That's Cisco," he said in a loud voice. "How come you killed him, Sam?"

"He was doin' his doggone best to kill me." Sam kept his voice mild. "Him and the other feller layin' over in the yard there."

The town marshal grunted, strode to the dead man, gave the corpse a brief glance.

"This here feller's Red Cotter." His voice was angry, belligerent. "Cole Garson ain't goin' to like this business, Sam. You killin' his men just because they figgered to sleep in your hotel."

"I reckon you got the wrong angle, Cliff." Sam's voice was dangerously soft. "These skunks wasn't figgerin' to do any sleepin' here."

"I should throw you in jail," blustered the town marshal. "Cole Garson's a big taxpayer. He'll want this thing investigated."

Sam said in the same soft voice, "Mebbe Garson would rather you'd keep your mouth shut, Cliff."

The town marshal seemed suddenly thoughtful. He rubbed a bristly chin, looked inquiringly at Ed Yate, as if for support.

The cattleman shook his head. "I'd go slow if I were you, Cliff," he said. "Must be some good reason why Sam used his gun on these men."

Sam looked at him, not quite pleased by something in his former employer's voice. He said, gruffly, "I've a notion you'll find they've got broncs cached close in the chaparral. They wouldn't cache their broncs in the brush if they figgered to bunk down in the hotel. They'd put up at Ben's barn like they always does when they hit town."

"I'll go see," Ben Wire said. He vanished in the chaparral, and in a moment his voice came back to them. "You're doggone right, Sam. Both their broncs cached back here."

Sam nodded, his face grim. "Ain't figgered it out yet." His gaze was hard on Ed Yate. "I seen 'em from up on the bluffs when I come over the ridge. From the way they come sneakin' out of the chaparral I kind of got the idee there was a killin' in their minds." He shook his head. "There don't seem no other answer."

The town marshal attempted more bluster. "We only got your word for it."

Sam was looking at the wounded man. Cisco's eyes were open. He seemed to be listening. Sam bent low over him, his big frame covering him for the moment from the view of the other men.

The look in the man's eyes told him that Doc Brown was going to be of little use. There was something, a desperate appeal there.

Sam said, in a whisper that only Cisco could hear, "Talk fast, feller, before it's too late."

Cisco's breath was coming in rasping gasps. Sam bent closer, gaze on the fluttering lips that were trying to form words.

The dying man's head suddenly lifted, and he said distinctly, "The gal, she's —" His head dropped, he shuddered, lay motionless.

Sam got up from his knees and the moonlight showed dread on his face.

"You heard him, Ed?" He was looking at the tall cowman. "Cisco died with somethin' bad on his mind. He wasn't likin' it, dyin' with this bad thing on his mind."

Ed Yate nodded, his face grave. "Something about a girl, wasn't it, Sam?"

"Yes," Sam said. "Something about a gal." His face was gray, haggard. "I've a notion I savvy what he meant, Ed, and I ain't likin' it."

"What did he mean?" asked Yate, his face puzzled.

Sam said, wearily, "I reckon we'd best talk it over private, Ed. There's been a lot goin' on you ain't had no chance to hear about."

Ben Wire appeared from the chaparral with the dead men's horses. "I'll put 'em up at the barn," he told Sam. "Reckon Garson will be sendin' in for 'em." He passed on to the street, the horses trailing on a rope.

The group of men from the dance hall were fading into the night. Ed Yate's look followed them.

"Got in town late," he said to Sam. "I was playing poker over in Vince's place when I heard the shots." He hesitated, showed embarrassment. "I'll see you later, Sam. Right now I'm going back and cash in my chips. I was sure guessing the cards right tonight." He hurried away.

Willie Logan came up on the run, the shotgun still clutched in his hands. "Doc's comin'." He stared with bulging eyes at the dead Bar G man. "Gosh, Sam, what were they after?"

Sam gave him an odd look. "Looks like they was after your skelp, son. Won't know for sure until you and me has done some talkin'."

The young hotel clerk gaped at him. "After me?"

"Chances are plenty good they was, Willie." There was grimness in Sam's faint smile. "Good thing I come along when I did."

The doctor hurried into the yard, a bag in his hand. He gave Red a brief glance, moved quickly for a look at Cisco.

"Got me out of bed for nothing," he grumbled. "These men will never be more dead."

"Sorry, Doc." Sam's tone was apologetic. "Cisco just cashed in."

Doc Brown gestured impatiently. "Well, no use for me to waste time here." He went off, muttering under his breath.

The town marshal paced uneasily back and forth between the two bodies. Sam watched him, his expression grim.

"Don't want 'em layin' here, Cliff," he finally commented. "Better get your wagon and haul 'em away."

The town marshal whirled on him. "You ain't heard the last of this business."

"There's more folks than me ain't heard the last of it," drawled Sam.

Cliff Burl glowered, rage and something like fear on his heavy face. He swung on his heel, stamped off toward the street.

Sam looked at Willie Logan. "All right, son. Let's go inside. I can see you've got plenty you want to tell me." He broke off, slapped a thigh. "Clean forgot my bronc. Looks like he wasn't waitin' for me to get him."

The horse came up at a slow trot, head high to keep the dangling reins from under his hoofs. He swerved from Sam's reaching hand, broke into a lope and disappeared inside the barn.

"You get back to the desk," Sam said. "Be with you quick as I strip off his saddle and shake some hay down for him." He paused, eyes on the shotgun in Willie's hands, added kindly, "You got plenty guts, son." His voice grew reproving. "Only next time you hear shootin', take it more careful. If it had been Cisco or Red standin' here when you come busting round the corner you'd have been as dead as they are now."

Willie Logan gave him a grin. There was a hint of a swagger in his walk as he made for the hotel porch.

Several of the guests were crowded around the desk firing questions at him when Sam rejoined him. Willie threw him a harassed look.

Sam grinned. Willie Logan was learning things about the hotel business, such as finding diplomatic answers for disturbed and worried guests.

He said, mildly, "It's all over, gents. The town marshal has got things in hand. There won't be no more shootin'."

The guests went tramping up the stairs. Willie surrendered the desk chair to his boss. He asked worriedly, "What for you think they were after me, Sam?"

"I reckon you mebbe savvy better than I do, son." Sam was watching him intently. "You heard what Cisco said just when he cashed in."

"Something about a girl." Willie's face was the color of the clean, white collar around his long neck. "My gosh, Sam. It's got me scared."

"Go on, son," encouraged Sam. "No sense wastin' time."

"Mary Carroll was in here," Willie told him. "About sundown. She looked awful, asked for you, said her dad was in bad trouble."

Sam nodded somberly. He was wishing he had not delayed his return from the hideout cabin in Bear Canyon. He had waited, hoping King Malory would show up. It seemed he had waited too long.

"She said Garson's outfit was at the ranch, had a row with her dad and took him off to Garson's place." Willie gulped. "Vince Lestang came in while she was talking. He said he would jump right out to Bar G and tell Garson to turn her dad loose."

"Mary went with him, huh?" Sam's big hand was clenched so tight the knuckles showed white.

Willie nodded miserably. "That's right."

The screen door slammed and Ben Wire hurried across the lobby. His face wore a grim look.

"Sam," the liveryman spoke in a rasping whisper, "I heard them words Cisco said and I know damn well what he meant. He was trying to tell about Mary Carroll. She went off at sundown with Vince Lestang."

"I reckon that's the answer, Ben." Despair made Sam's voice hoarse.

"Mighty queer he wanted you to know," wondered the liveryman. "Cisco and Red were both of 'em killin' wolves."

Sam said somberly, "Some folks get that way when they feel death on 'em. I reckon death touched the one decent spark in him. He was worried about her, and that means —" His voice choked.

Willie Logan broke the brief silence. "I want to know why you think they came gunning for me. It doesn't make sense."

Sam's fingers drummed on the desk. "Makes plenty sense. Garson wasn't wantin' it known she left town with Vince Lestang."

Ben Wire nodded. "That's the answer, Sam," he agreed.

Willie studied their grave faces with puzzled eyes. "I don't get you," he muttered.

Sam explained patiently, "They figgered you was the only one who'd know she'd gone off to Garson's ranch." He looked at the liveryman. "You and Ben," he added softly.

Ben Wire nodded again. "That's right, Sam. Me and Willie both was on that murder tally."

The expression on Willie's face showed he quite understood now. He gave Sam a wild look, went shakily to a chair and slumped into it.

Ben Wire shook his head gloomily. "Looks awful bad for Mary and her pa. Wish I was sheriff ag'in. I'd round up a posse and go after 'em."

Sam said nothing. He was wondering what had become of King Malory. He was longing desperately for King Malory at this moment.

CHAPTER
SIXTEEN

A Gray Dawn

The sounds drifted into the cabin, faint stirrings on the night wind that made Pete Walker reach hastily for his boots. He dragged them on, buckled gun belt over lean hips, snatched up his rifle and hurried outside.

He had not been mistaken. Horses approaching up the trail. He would see them when they angled around the cliff and crossed the moonlit wash a hundred yards below the cabin.

Thankful that he had always been a light sleeper, Pete moved swiftly into the brush, crouched in the deep shadows, rifle ready. The approach of a single horseman would not have unduly alarmed him. They had been expecting King Malory to show up. The hoof thuds told him that several riders were in the party. Might be that trouble was coming.

He kept his gaze fastened on the strip of dry wash where moonlight lay bright, and now he saw them, three horsemen. Relief put a grin on his face. The rider in the lead was King, and he had old Jim Carroll with him. The third rider made him narrow his eyes. He'd seen him in town, a Bar G man he knew as Sandy

185

Wells. Mighty queer King would bring a Bar G man to the hideout cabin. Wasn't a prisoner either. No sign of a rope on him.

He continued to wait in the concealment of the brush, uncertain now, and aware of vague, disturbing doubts.

The three men halted their horses and King slid from his saddle, stood looking at the dark cabin. Moonlight touched his face. He looked tired, relaxed, like a man who now felt no need to be on the alert for danger. His manner indicated a certain confidence of security here.

Pete was not taking chances. He had to be sure. He spoke softly. "I've got you covered, fellers. Be awful careful."

Carroll and the Bar G man stiffened in their saddles, and King said quickly, "Take it easy, Sandy." His voice loudened. "It's all right, Pete."

"I'm cravin' to know how come you fetched this Bar G coyote along with you."

"Sandy's quit Bar G, Pete." Grim amusement touched King's voice. "He's on our side now."

Pete stepped from the dark bushes. "Wasn't takin' chances, King." He glanced at Jim Carroll. "Looks like you've pulled off some fancy play."

"I'll say he has." Sandy Wells grinned at him. "He's my boss now, feller." He dropped from his saddle. "I sure like his style."

Jim Carroll got down stiffly. "You or Sam been in town today, Pete?" He asked the question anxiously.

Pete shook his head. "Sam headed for town an hour ago." He looked at King. "He waited for you to show up. You didn't show, so he forked saddle for town."

"I was hoping you'd heard word of my girl." Jim Carroll spoke despondently.

Pete eyed him shrewdly. It was obvious a lot of things had been happening and that Mary Carroll's whereabouts was important. He said, an attempt at reassurance in his voice, "Sam will likely run into her at the hotel. I wouldn't get to frettin', Jim."

Mary's father was silent, worried gaze on King who suddenly began stripping the saddle off the buckskin.

"I'm needing a fresh horse, Pete," he said laconically.

"Headin' for town right off?" asked Pete.

"I want to see Sam and get in touch with Ed Yate, if possible."

Pete frowned, looked doubtfully at Carroll and Sandy. "They savvy about you?"

King nodded. "I had to tell them, Pete. Things have been moving too fast for me to keep them in the dark. It seemed best to tell them." He grinned. "Jim knows where we've cached his cows."

"I'll get a rope on Silver King," Pete said briskly.

"I'm needing a fresh horse myself," Jim Carroll told him.

"No need for you to go with me," demurred King.

"I'm ridin' with you," stubbornly insisted Carroll. "I want to know about my girl."

King saw that argument was useless. "All right, fix him up, Pete."

187

"Ain't needin' no fresh bronc," Sandy announced. "Reckon this roan of mine's got plenty life in him yet."

"You're staying here," drawled King.

Disappointment showed on the cowboy's face. "I figgered to ride along with you," he protested.

"Who did you say your boss is now?" King asked him good-naturedly.

Sandy grinned. "All right, boss. If you say I'm stayin', I ain't sayin' different."

"You can tell Pete about the way you said *adios* to Garson," smiled King.

"Sure will," chuckled the cowboy.

Pete came up with the two fresh horses. "You throw on the saddles," he told Sandy. "I'll fix up a pot of coffee."

"No time to waste with coffee," fretted Jim Carroll.

King looked at him. The rancher was in bad shape. Worry for Mary was getting him down.

"All right, Pete." King's tone was firm. "You fix up that coffee and a couple of sandwiches."

He shot questions at Pete while they drank the coffee, learned about the little-used trail by which they could reach the barn in the rear of the hotel.

"I don't want to run into your town marshal," King said.

"Cliff Burl most always hangs about in the Border Palace this time of night," Pete reassured. "You can get into the hotel easy the back way. Two doors there. The small one opens into my room. Jim and you can hole up there until you get hold of Sam. His room is next to mine. He'll likely have hit the hay, time you make town.

Ain't no chance you can overtake him, not with the hour's start he's got."

The moon was directly overhead by the time they reached the bluffs and glimpsed the hotel. The two men reined their horses, and Jim Carroll said hopefully, "Looks quiet enough down there." His gaze was on the yellow glow in the lobby windows. "We'll soon know if she's there." His voice cracked. "My God! She's got to be there!"

Another fifteen minutes found them down in the chaparral and close to the barn. They led the horses inside, tied them, left the saddles on. A horse nickered softly from an adjoining stall. King took a look, recognized the big rangy bay. Sam Doan's horse — and that indicated Sam was somewhere inside the hotel.

Silent, watchful, they crossed the path of moonlit yard, and found the small door Pete said would open into his room. King carefully inserted the key Pete had given him. The lock turned with a click startlingly loud in the stillness.

He waited a moment, listening, then slowly inched the door open and stepped into the dark room. Jim Carroll followed. Excitement made the rancher clumsy and his foot stubbed against a chair. It toppled over, hit something that gave a sharp tinny sound. A bucket, or perhaps Pete's spittoon, King guessed. He grasped Carroll's arm, held him quiet.

A minute passed. They heard a movement in the adjoining room, saw a thin line of lamplight under the door. It was evident the crash had been heard.

King took a chance, spoke softly, "Sam!"

The movement in the room beyond ceased. There was a silence, and then a low whisper, close to the door.

"That you, Pete?"

Sam Doan's voice. King relaxed his grip on Carroll's arm, spoke more loudly. "It's all right, Sam. Open the door and give us some light."

The door opened, revealed Sam, a lantern dangling from steel hook, a gun in his good hand. He gave them an amazed look, came into the room, set the lantern on the floor and closed the door.

"I'll be doggoned!" He was staring at Jim Carroll. "Thought you was at Bar G and a rope reachin' for you." His dazed look went to King. "How come, son?"

Jim Carroll took a step toward him. "Mary here?" His voice was unsteady.

The expression on Sam's face was answer enough. The brief hope faded from the rancher's eyes. He stood there stunned, unable to speak, his face a haggard, dreadful mask of despair.

Sam was finding words. "Mary went out to Bar G with Vince Lestang to get you away from there." His voice ended in a groan. "My God, if this ain't hell." His frowning gaze fastened again on King. "How come you got Jim away, fetched him here?" he repeated.

King explained briefly. Sam nodded, said sorrowfully, "I reckon you'd left by the time Vince and Mary got there." He shook his head. "A hell of a business."

King was recalling Sandy's words after his look into the ranchyard. *It's Lestang. Had a fellow with him. Couldn't see him good. Too dark under the trees.* He had never felt so heartsick. Lestang's companion must

190

have been Mary Carroll. Obviously, she had not been wearing skirts and Sandy's mistake was natural enough. Sam was right. It was a hell of a business. Mary Carroll had walked into that house at the very moment of her father's escape.

Sam moved over from the door, uprighted the tin can knocked over by the chair, an improvised spittoon made from a five gallon coal oil container. He said, in his slow voice, "Nabbed a couple of fellers when I came in awhile back. Bar G hombres, name of Cisco and Red. Looks like they come sneakin' in to empty some lead into Willie Logan, and mebbe hand the same to Ben Wire."

King waited, silent, grim. Sam gave Jim Carroll a pitying look.

"Seems like Willie and Ben was the only two people in San Lucas as knowed that Mary went off with Vince Lestang. I reckon you can figger the answer for yourself, King. Means Garson and Lestang wasn't wantin' it known about Mary."

"There's no other answer." King wondered at the sound of his voice. It was like another man speaking, a hard, savage, snarling voice. He fought for self-control, added quietly, "You mean you got the jump on 'em, huh, Sam."

"Didn't want 'em layin' in my yard messin' the scenery," Sam told him bleakly. "I told Cliff Burl to haul 'em off to his Boothill." His smile came, hard, bitter. "Cliff wasn't likin' it much, and was all set to throw me in jail. Kind of had to get tough with the

191

skunk, and then Ed Yate got rough with him, sent him off with his tail awful low."

King's eyes narrowed. "You mean Ed Yate is in town now?"

"Settin' in the lobby," Sam told him. "Him and me and Ben Wire is havin' a powwow, figgerin' what to do about Mary." He sidled a brief glance at Jim Carroll. "It was in my mind Ed Yate could do somethin'."

Jim Carroll came out of his daze. He turned to the yard door. "I'm going back to Bar G. I'm killing Lestang with my bare hands."

King stepped in front of him, said in a harsh voice, "Use your head, Carroll."

The half-crazed rancher's hand went down to the gun in his holster. King grasped his wrist. "Use your head," he repeated. His voice softened, "Don't make things worse for Mary."

Carroll's big shoulders sagged. "Reckon I'm loco. I was seeing red for a moment."

Sam Doan reached his steel hook for the lantern. "Let me tell you somethin', Jim." His tone was solemn. "Next to God thar's only one feller I know of as can help Mary right now, and that's King Malory. I knowed his granddad, and the boy here is old King's fightin' self and packs more brains in his head than Garson ever heard of."

Jim Carroll stared at him. His expression was odd, almost a grimace. "You don't need to tell me about King. I've seen him in action."

King said, a mingling of amusement and annoyance in his voice, "Let's join that powwow."

They followed him into the next room which opened into the hall leading to the lobby. The berserk fury that had ravaged Carroll's face was gone. He gave Sam a hard, cool smile, and Sam grinned back at him.

Something like a frown darkened Ed Yate's face when he saw King. It was gone in an instant and he jerked upright from his chair, hand outstretched, his smile friendly.

Apparently, King did not see the reaching hand. He was looking at Ben Wire whose own hand had closed over the gun in his holster. There was startled recognition in the ex-sheriff's shrewd eyes. He had seen the picture in the Santa Fé *Republican*, read the account of the notorious border outlaw.

Sam shook his head at him, grinned. "Ben, meet King Malory, special investigator for the San Lucas Stockmen's Association."

Another frown briefly shadowed Ed Yate's face. His hand dropped and he settled down in his chair. "Not your business, Sam, telling Ben the truth about King." Resentment edged his voice.

Sam scowled back at him. "You're damn wrong, Ed, claimin' King ain't my business." His tone was brittle. "Ain't never liked this crazy business no time. Got a bad smell to it."

Ed Yate's hand lifted, a lazy, good-natured gesture. "Always easy to get you on the prod, Sam." He was looking at Jim Carroll, a hard, speculative curiosity in his eyes. "I thought you were some kind of prisoner out at Garson's place, Jim." He smiled. "It seems the story was all wrong."

"You heard the story right, Ed." Carroll spoke quietly. "I've a good idea I'd be dead by now if King hadn't got me away from there." His voice hardened. "The story's a lot worse now. You've heard about Vince Lestang taking my girl out there."

Yate nodded. "I wouldn't worry too much about her, Jim." He shrugged. "I'm not meaning I like or trust Cole Garson. He's bad to the bone." The Flying Y man looked significantly at King. "Shouldn't wonder but what Malory picked up a warm trail out at Bar G. You know now that the Association hired him to track down the man who's bossing this rustler gang."

Ben Wire shook off the daze brought on by the discovery of King's identity. He said bitterly, "You wouldn't be needin' no special investigator if you'd re-elected me as sheriff. It's your fault, Ed, workin' like you done to get me throwed out of office."

"Still spreading that crazy story around." Yate shook his head reproachfully. "Don't blame me, Ben. It boils down to the fact that a lot of cattlemen had the idea you were too old for the job of running down the brains of the gang. I had to ride along with the majority or get in bad."

Ben's indignant snort indicated his disbelief. Yate returned his attention to Carroll. "What I was getting at, when Ben interrupted me, is that while I don't much trust Garson, I do trust Vince Lestang. He's a responsible citizen in this town. Your daughter is safe enough with him and you have no need to worry." The cattleman paused, gestured. "It's not logical to think he'd turn round and bring her back at this late hour.

194

He'd wait until morning." Yate nodded confidently. "She'll be back in town by noon, Carroll. Vince won't let the girl come to harm."

There was a silence, broken by King's voice, quiet, hard. "We don't want to wait until morning, Mr. Yate. You see, we have reason to believe you have things sized up all wrong."

The frown on Ed Yate's face was real enough now. He said half angrily, "We don't even know for sure that the girl is at Garson's place."

"Willie Logan and Ben was awful sure that's where she went with Vince Lestang," gruffly reminded Sam.

"Vince could have taken her out to your own ranch," Yate suggested to Carroll.

"No use talkin'," rasped Sam. "Willie heard 'em say here in this office they was headin' for Bar G, and that's where they went."

Yate's smile was back, friendly, sympathetic as he looked at their stern faces. "I was only trying to keep Jim Carroll from worrying too much." His tone was soothing. "If Vince took the girl out to Garson's place, there is no reason to think he won't bring her back in the morning."

"You're wrong again, Yate." The hardness in King's voice was more pronounced, drew their eyes. "Garson sent two men here to kill Willie Logan and Ben Wire. Can you explain that away?"

Yate was silent and there was a hint of uneasiness in his narrowed eyes. He fingered nervously in a pocket, drew out a cigar, chewed off the end and lit it.

King continued in the same hard voice. "The fact that Garson planned to kill the only two people who would know Mary Carroll had gone to the ranch with Lestang certainly proves that she is still there. It also seems to prove that Lestang is mixed up in the affair." King shook his head. "No use fooling ourselves. Lestang has no intentions of bringing Mary Carroll back to this town tomorrow or any other time."

Yate chewed thoughtfully on the cigar, suddenly dropped it in the spittoon and got out of his chair. "Only one way to settle it," he said resignedly. "Get out to Garson's ranch."

"Now?" demanded Jim Carroll. Excitement fired his eyes.

"Now," agreed the Flying Y man. "Just as quick as Ben can get my team hitched."

"I'm going along," declared Mary's father.

"Suit yourself." Yate's look was on King. "You'll join the party, Malory?"

King shook his head. "No."

"Afraid, huh?" The tall cowman's smile was insolent. "You've talked me into it, Malory. Seems fair enough for you to come along."

"You don't know what's been going on at the Garson ranch." King spoke quietly. "Garson doesn't love me much after what I did to him."

"I'm not afraid of the polecat," Carroll said impatiently. "Let's get going, Ed."

"You're not going with him, Jim," interrupted King. "It would only make matters worse."

"My girl's out there," fumed Carroll.

"Use your head." King's tone was patient, as if arguing with a recalcitrant child. "Getting yourself killed won't help Mary."

"You listen to King," urged Sam. "He's talkin' good sense. Garson ain't forgettin' what him and you done to him."

"I'll get the team hitched," Ben Wire said. He hurried into the night.

Sam was watching King intently. He apparently caught the thought in the younger man's mind. King wanted somebody to accompany Yate.

Sam reached for his hat. "I'll go along with you, Ed," he said. A grim smile spread over his face. "Garson ain't knowin' yet about Cisco and Red."

"Garson wouldn't do a thing about it if he did know," King reassured him. "He wouldn't admit that he knew Cisco and Red were here on a killing job." King gave Yate a covert glance. "Garson likes to keep his shirt clean. He's an important man — a member of the Stockmen's Association."

Ed Yate reached inside a pocket for a fresh cigar. He lit it, puffed out a cloud of smoke that veiled the sharp look he darted at the Association's special investigator.

He said blandly, "Thanks, Sam. I want you along. Good idea in case we don't find Carroll's girl at the ranch. Your word is good with Carroll or anybody else in this town."

"Damn it, Ed!" Carroll's face reddened. "I haven't said your word wouldn't be good!"

"A witness is a good thing to have along," smiled the tall cowman. "I gather from the talk that Garson is

197

hostile to both Malory and yourself." He looked at King through curling cigar smoke. "Wouldn't have been a bad idea if you'd killed the old wolf."

King returned the look steadily, his face expressionless. "Garson offered me a job," he said. "He didn't like me turning him down in spite of the fact that he believes the story that I'm an outlaw. He said he could protect me, hide me out from the law."

"That's bad, Malory." The Flying Y man's tone was grave. "I hate to think a member of our Association is one of the rustler gang, perhaps the sly fox we want you to catch. It's possible you've picked up a clue there, Malory."

King made no reply. He was thinking of something Manuel had said. *There is one who comes. A tall man with gray in his hair.* King was conscious of cold prickles as he gazed at Ed Yate. The thing that kept creeping into his mind was absurd, a nightmarish fancy.

He heard Yate's voice, friendly, hearty, "Well, Sam, let's go see if Ben's got the buckboard ready." He lifted a hand at King and Carroll, strode toward the door.

King's look held Sam back for a moment. "Jim and I will be waiting with Pete. Savvy?"

Sam nodded. "Savvy," he said.

He was gone before another thought came to King. He had promised himself to ask Sam about the ownership of the buckskin horse. Too late now. There were reasons why it seemed best not to question Sam about the buckskin in front of Ed Yate. The matter would have to wait.

198

He felt Jim Carroll's eyes on him, gave the worried rancher his slow smile, warm, encouraging. This man was the father of the girl he loved. Waiting was going to be hard for both of them. He yearned just as greatly as Jim Carroll to be riding for Bar G, and it had not been easy to choose not to go. An alternative decision would have meant sure disaster. He wanted to be alive, bring these men to swift justice, avenge Mary if harm had been done her.

He said, "Well, Jim, no use our sticking around. Might as well get our horses and head back to Bear Canyon."

Jim Carroll said gloomily, "I reckon that's right." And followed him down the hall and out to the yard by way of Pete's room. Dawn showed pale above the eastern mountains. King wondered grimly what the new day would bring.

CHAPTER
SEVENTEEN

Trail to Los Higos

There was good reason for the solemn look on Sam Doan's face. He dreaded having to tell Jim Carroll that the trip to Bar G had drawn a blank. Jim would take it hard and no blame to him. King was going to be mighty upset, too. The news was going to hurt him plenty. Only he wouldn't act loco about it like Jim. He'd keep his head, set his brains to working.

There were other reasons for Sam's low spirits. He was dog-tired, red-eyed for want of sleep. He had wasted no time after getting back to town, had thrown on saddle and headed straight for the Bear Canyon cabin.

Pete saw him coming, His shrill yell brought the others in a rush. They stood there silent, eyes questioning as he rode up and halted the sweating bay horse under the tall trees.

The grim look on his face was enough. Jim Carroll went rigid. He spoke, his voice an agonized whisper. "Sam, she — she's dead?"

Sam was weary to the point of collapse, his nerves on edge, jumpy. It was an effort to keep his voice quiet. No sense wasting words answering wild questions.

200

He fixed red-rimmed eyes on King. "Couldn't find no trace of Mary at Bar G," he said. "Garson claims she never showed up at the ranch."

"She's dead," groaned Jim.

Sam slid stiffly from his saddle, faced him, growing irritation plain on his tired face. "It won't do no good actin' loco," he grumbled. "Just because Mary ain't at Garson's place don't mean she's dead."

Carroll clenched big hands. "I should have gone myself."

King interrupted his outburst. "Sam is talking good sense, Jim. It won't do Mary any good for you to lose your head."

Something in his voice seemed to steady the distraught rancher. His hands unclenched, and after a moment he said quietly, "All right, Sam. Let's have the story."

"Ain't really no story," Sam told them. "Like I said, Mary wasn't at the ranch no place. Ed Yate talked plenty rough to Garson, made him take us all over. Questioned the whole doggone outfit. All the boys backed up Garson, swore Mary hadn't showed up no time."

King asked softly, "How about Vince Lestang?"

Sam shook his head. "He wasn't there. Garson said he'd gone back to town. Kind of queer we didn't meet him on the road."

King thought it over, a frown on his face. "He could have been there, hiding out from you."

"Waal," Sam spoke doubtfully, "ain't sayin' you're wrong. His team was gone. He was drivin' them Morgans of his and they wasn't in the barn."

King asked sharply, "Was Ed Yate with you when you took that look in the barn?"

Sam shook his head again, a hint of worry in his eyes. "Left Ed back in the house, talkin' with Garson. It was Dal Santeen took me over to the barn when I asked to see if the Morgans was there."

Pete said thoughtfully, "If Vince had headed for town you and Ed would sure have met him on the road."

"That's right." Sam felt in his shirt pocket, drew out a crumpled sheet of paper. "Found this layin' on the table over to your place, Jim. We dropped in on the way back to town. I thought mebbe we'd find Mary there." He flapped a limp hand. "She wasn't there, only this piece of paper."

"Let me have it." King held out a hand, read the scrawl aloud.

YOU'RE NOT SO SMART, MALORY. YOU GOT THE FATHER, BUT WE GOT THE GIRL. I'LL TRADE HER FOR YOU. THE GIRL CAN KEEP THE FATHER.

"The skunk," muttered Pete Walker. He scowled at his partner. "Looks like Mary's still there at Bar. G, Sam."

"Ed Yate figgered it was a trick to get King high-tailin' it over that way," Sam answered. "Ed says King would be plumb loco to be fooled by that piece of paper now we know for sure Mary ain't at the ranch."

Jim Carroll broke his morose silence. "I'm throwing a saddle on my horse. I don't care what Garson does to me, if he'll turn my girl loose."

"You won't find her at Garson's place," King told him. "The best thing you can do is to stay right here."

"Meaning what?" flared the rancher.

"Meaning that a wrong move at this time will not bring Mary back. You're in no shape to think it out straight, Jim."

"You'll do the thinking for me, huh?" fumed Mary's father.

"Yes," drawled King, "you've said it."

Sam, watching him, was conscious of the thrill he had felt when this calm-eyed grandson of old King Malory stepped from the Deming stage. There was again the same formidable something that cloaked him like shining armor, a resolute courage that no odds could dismay.

He said softly, "King's right, Jim."

"We'll not sit here and wait for miracles," King assured Carroll. His eyes narrowed thoughtfully at Sam. "Who owns the buckskin Ed Yate turned over to me?"

Sam showed surprise. "Ed owns him," he answered.

"Sure does," confirmed Pete. "That buckskin was foaled out at Flyin' Y and it was me broke him to saddle."

"What for you want to know?" asked Sam, deeply puzzled by the curious speculation in King's eyes.

King's face hardened. He was recalling more words from Manuel. *This one is like the buckskin horse the*

tall gray man was riding the last time he make the visit.
No doubts left now. Manuel's *rico* was Ed Yate.

The knowledge crystallized ugly doubts into uglier
suspicions. He crumpled the piece of paper Sam had
brought from the Carroll ranch, dropped it, and gave
Sam a grim look.

"Was it Yate's idea for you to ride over to the Carroll
ranch?"

"Sure was." Sam nodded. "Ed figgered we'd mebbe
find Mary hidin' there."

"And he thought this note was bait to get me out to
Bar G?"

"That's the way Ed looked at it," answered Sam.
"Said you'd be a fool to fall for it, but reckoned you'd
be fool enough to go." The expression in King's eyes
worried Sam. "I reckon you ain't the fool Ed figgers,"
he added. "You wouldn't last no time a-tall if you let
that bait hook you, son."

King was silent, evidently thinking it over. He said
finally, "It's my guess Mary was at the ranch when you
and Yate looked the place over. Lestang, too."

"Ain't sayin' you're wrong." Sam looked dubious.
"Garson could have fooled us."

"We'll say he fooled you," King said dryly.

Sam's head perked up. "Meanin' Ed wasn't fooled?"
he asked in a startled voice.

"I'll make another guess," continued King. "Mary
and Lestang are not at the ranch now. So don't worry.
I'm not picking up Garson's bait." He paused, added
thoughtfully. "Where would Lestang take Mary if he
didn't take her back to San Lucas?"

Sam and Pete exchanged looks, and Sam said, his voice slow, troubled, "Why, I reckon he'd take her someplace where we wouldn't think to look."

"Someplace a good ways off from San Lucas," commented Pete.

"Like down below the border," suggested King.

Sam nodded. "It was in my mind thataways."

Sandy Wells muttered an exclamation. "Listen," he said. "I'm bettin' on Los Higos. There's an old Comanchero road runs most all the way from the ranch. Lestang knows that road like he knows his own face."

"You know that road?" asked King.

"I'll say I do." The cowboy gave him a bitter smile. "Anybody works for Garson gets to know that road awful well trailin' cows to the border."

"Bar G cows?" Sam eyed him suspiciously.

"I ain't talkin' about cows," coolly reminded the cowboy. "I'm talkin' about where I think Lestang has took the Carroll girl."

King gave Sam a warning shake of the head. "Sandy is all right," he said. "Sandy's on my payroll now." He smiled encouragingly at the former Bar G man. "You know Los Higos?"

"Sure do." Sandy's resentment faded. "Speak Spanish, too." He grinned. "Them señoritas can learn a feller the lingo awful fast."

"Fine." Excitement glinted in King's eyes. "You go throw on saddles. I'm taking you along with me."

Sandy hesitated. "You want the buckskin?"

King gave Sam a bleak smile. "You can turn that buckskin loose in the basin. He'll be safe there until I want him."

Sandy was waiting, his face puzzled. King said, "I'm riding Silver King this time. Make it fast, feller. We're leaving here on the jump."

The cowboy hurried away, and Sam said in a mystified voice. "Don't savvy what's on your mind, son. How come you want to cache Ed's buckskin down in the basin, and what for was you askin' about who owned him?"

King said wearily. "I'm using my head for something else than a hat peg, Sam."

Sam rubbed a massive nose reflectively with his steel hook. "There's things I don't savvy, son." His tone was troubled. "I've been doin' some thinkin' and what I think don't make sense. I've a notion Ben Wire gets to wonderin' about Ed Yate the same way."

Amazement spread over Jim Carroll's face. "You're crazy," he told them angrily. "Ed Yate is the biggest man in the San Lucas country, head of the Stockmen's Association, a rich man. You can't drag him into this business."

"Just talkin' aloud, Jim," drawled Sam. "At that there's an awful lot you don't know about. Like I said, Ben Wire and me has plenty reasons to get notions, and I reckon King has been puttin' some pieces together and ain't likin' the picture." He gave King a grim nod. "All right, son. We'll keep that buckskin horse safe for you."

206

Sandy came up with the horses, helped Pete fill and tie on canteens.

"I should be riding with you," grumbled Mary's father.

King climbed into his saddle, looked at him sympathetically. "It's mighty hard on you, Jim, waiting and wondering. It's better this way, just Sandy with me. Too many of us would attract attention and we can't afford the risk. Sandy knows his way around in that Mexican town and he speaks Spanish. He's the man to go with me." He paused, added softly, "Mary's life and more is at stake, Jim. Don't forget that, and don't you leave this place, or you'll only make things a lot harder."

They went down the trail. The big, cream-colored horse was full of life. King held him to a fast shuffling walk. He did not speak, only nodded when Sandy indicated the trail that would take them over the first ridge. He was thinking of Manuel, wondering if he would find him at the *cantina* of his uncle, Francisco Cota. Manuel was going to be more valuable than he knew. He must manage to have Manuel get a look at Ed Yate. It was of vital importance to have Yate identified as the tall, gray man whose habit of surreptitiously visiting Bar G at night had aroused the Mexican's curiosity.

He broke his silence. "Ever see Ed Yate at Bar G?" he asked Sandy.

The cowboy shook his head. "Never seen him out at the ranch no time."

"You know him when you see him?"

"Sure I do. Seen him plenty times in town. Ain't many folks in San Lucas don't know Ed Yate when they see him."

"You wouldn't know for a fact he's never been out to see Garson," argued King.

"That's right. There's always folks that drop in after dark. Not my business. Never paid no attention." Sandy grinned. "Garson wasn't likin' it for us to be nosy. We wasn't wanted hangin' round the big house. Was different with Santeen and Cisco and Red. Them fellers was most always close to the boss. I reckon they could tell plenty." The cowboy paused, added grimly, "No chance now to get any talk from Cisco and Red. Not without we follow 'em down to hell."

"You know the *cantina* of Francisco Cota?" King asked him.

"Sure do." Sandy chuckled. "Francisco's a big fat hombre. He's uncle to the Mex feller that hightailed it away from Bar G yesterday. Sure I know that *cantina*." His voice faded on a reminiscent note.

"We're going there," King said.

Sandy looked pleased, and a bit regretful. He was thinking of Francisco Cota's pretty niece. The thought of seeing Juanita stirred pleasant emotions. She was a señorita with plenty of snap. What caused his momentary gloom was the grim certainty he would have little or no time for making love to Francisco Cota's languishing-eyed niece.

They turned into the old road rutted deep by many a Comanchero *carreta* carrying goods from Old Mexico into the Indian country to be exchanged for loot, stolen cattle and horses.

Stolen cattle were still being trailed over this same ancient road, King reflected grimly. When the time was ripe he would ask Sandy Wells to tell him what he knew about it.

Sandy said, "Should make Los Higos by the time the moon's up."

The road leveled out. They put their horses to an easy lope.

CHAPTER
EIGHTEEN

A Silver Buckle

Manuel Cota was not forgetting the Americano who had rescued him from a vile bondage, put gold pieces in his hand and called him *amigo*. They were *muy simpatico*.

The Mexican jingled the gold pieces in his pocket. He had promised the brave gringo to wait for him at the *cantina*, vowed also to be his eyes and his ears. It was plain that enemies sought the gringo's life. It was well to keep the flame of vigilance burning bright day and night, be alert for these *villanos* who sought to kill his friend and patron.

Manuel jingled the gold pieces again, a merry sound that pleased him. How his uncle's eyes had bulged in his fat face at the sight of this fine Americano gold. He had looked wise, frowned, sternly intimated that the money was the price of a stolen steer, then slyly suggested that Manuel let him keep it in a safe place for him. Manuel's refusal of the kind offer had made the old innkeeper quite angry. He had warned Manuel he would have only himself to blame if he awoke some morning and found his gold gone. A remark that decided Manual to sleep with one eye open during his stay in the *cantina* of his uncle, Francisco Cota.

Juanita, too, had chosen to make sly comments about his gold. Her brother must indeed be a *bandido* or perhaps he was now in the cattle business like her *vaquero* Americano. She had laughed, refused to believe Manuel's heated denial that he was a rustler like her yellow-haired gringo *amigo*.

Manuel's face took on a troubled look as he thought of Sandy Wells. The good-natured cowboy had been his one lone friend at Bar G ranch. He must be most careful if his new *amigo* Americano should ask questions. He had said he would soon come to Los Higos because he wanted to talk to Manuel, find out what he knew about affairs at Bar G ranch. He must not get Sandy into trouble. Sandy was his *amigo*, too, and in love with Juanita. He had more than once offered to help Manuel get away from the terrible old devil who held him in slavery because of a few paltry pesos. Manuel had always feared to run away. Cole Garson's arm was long, and Manuel had seen what happened to those who defied him.

Not even the pleasant jingle of gold in his pocket lightened the gloom on the Mexican's face as he reflected on Garson's long arm. It might even reach across the border, snatch him from his uncle's *cantina*. *Por Dios!* He must pray for the Americano's early arrival in Los Higos. The gringo was a man without fear. He would know what to do.

A haze of dust appeared in the distance. Manuel watched it lazily from his bench under the huge fig tree

211

in front of the *cantina* set well back from the road. There were many such fig trees in the street, venerable giants with interlacing branches that roofed out the sun. Manuel knew they had been planted by the padres in the long ago when they had reared the church in the little plaza. The church was now a ruin of crumbling adobe walls but the trees still bore eloquent testimony to the good works of those devout pioneering Franciscans. They bore fruit, too, and Manuel need only reach out a hand and pick up a luscious black fig that ripeness had sent tumbling to the ground. Each tree had its quota of grunting razor-backed pigs rooting for the fallen fruit.

The dust swirled, lifted, drew closer. Manuel's indolence left him. He forgot the fig he was reaching for. Somebody was in great haste to get to Los Higos, which was strange considering there was little in the squalid collection of adobe hovels to reward such haste. No doubt some gringo *bandido* in flight from above the border. Los Higos frequently had rascals of their breed as temporary citizens.

A long-legged sow grunted up, gave the interested young Mexican a wary look, then dashed at the big black fig at his feet. Manuel took no notice of the invasion. He was gazing increduously at the buckboard rattling up the rough street. The fine horses were in a lather of sweat. They had come a long way and traveled fast.

It was not the horses, though, that held his fascinated gaze. The driver was the elegant caballero he had sometimes seen at Bar G ranch. The one with the

212

waxed black mustache who had once tossed him a silver dollar. There was a señorita sitting by his side. She looked unhappy, like one very frightened. A slim girl with dark brown curls, and she wore the pants of a man. Strange people, these Americanos. No decent Mexican girl would wear the pants of a man. It was not modest.

Manuel was on his feet now, very still in the deep shade under the fig tree. Instinct warned him it would not be good for the gringo dandy to catch sight of him. He was a friend of Señor Garson, one of the mysterious men who came in stealth by night to visit the owner of Bar G. He might chance to recognize the Mexican to whom he had once tossed a silver dollar.

The tall trotters had slowed to a walk and the gringo was staring at the *cantina* as if it was in his mind to pull up under the shady trees and pause for a drink of wine. The girl's head lifted and Manuel felt her eyes on him. There was desperation in them, a mute appeal that was like a stab in his heart. *Verdad!* Something was very bad here. This girl was indeed frightened!

It was evident that the gringo dandy had abandoned the idea to pause for a glass of wine. He did not halt the team, but drove up the street, past the plaza, and pulled up in front of a long adobe building set back from the street in a little square shaded by great fig trees. El Gato's place!

Worry deepened in Manuel's eyes. El Gato was the richest man in Los Higos. He was also a very bad man, a *bandido*, it was rumored, which was why he was so rich and had such a grand place with bright yellow walls and the new roof of tiles that had come all the way from Mexico City. It was wicked of the gringo dandy to take this frightened girl to the house of El Gato. But no doubt the gringo was a very wicked man or he would not be friends with men like Señor Garson and El Gato.

Manuel considered the matter at length, came to the conclusion that he must do something about it. He had promised his good *amigo* Americano to be his eyes and his ears, and here was an affair that no doubt would deeply interest him. He must find out why the frightened girl should have been taken to a bad place like El Gato's house where desperados came from both sides of the border for wine, women, and the dance. He would use his eyes and his ears, and when his *amigo* Americano came, he would be able to act swiftly, save the frightened girl from the terrible claws of El Gato.

Manuel jingled his coins. The music of them warmed his courage. He sauntered into the yellowing light of the dusty street where life was beginning to stir with the approach of the cooling twilight. Girls appeared in gay, full-skirted dresses, strolled arm in arm in the plaza, laughing, chattering, casting demure glances at ogling youths, tossing shining black heads at too bold admirers.

Manuel moved among them, nonchalant, a bit wistful when he thought of the gold pieces in his pocket. It would be fun to spend his gold on one of these laughing-eyed señoritas. He resolutely downed the thought, gradually worked his way into the yard of El Gato.

214

A man was unhooking the fine bay horses from the gringo dandy's buckboard. Manuel gave him an amiable grin, paused, and began making a brown paper cigarette, his motions slow, indolent.

The man took the horses away. Manuel sauntered to a gnarled old fig tree, leaned against the trunk and put a match to his cigarette. He had the look of one who was lazily enjoying the cool of the evening, but the eyes under his steeple hat were slyly examining the upper balcony windows. The frightened señorita was very tired, and even a man like El Gato, whose heart was harder than stone, would want her to rest.

"He will not want her to look like a pale ghost," the Mexican reflected. "It would not be good for his vile business."

He continued to wait, eyes watchful, and Mary saw him lounging there under the fig tree. She stood at an open window which was barred with an iron grill. Beyond the window was a narrow balcony some three feet wide.

Her heart stood still. There was something familiar about the man down there. His face lifted again in a surreptitious look, and now she recognized him. The youth whose eyes had met hers as Lestang had slowed the team in front of the *cantina* down the street.

His furtive glances at the balcony windows meant he had guessed something was wrong and wanted to help her.

She tried desperately to think of something she could do to attract his attention, finally slipped a hand between the bars, wiggled it up and down. The

215

movement caught his eyes, and after a moment his own hand lifted in a cautious, answering signal.

Mary fluttered her hand again, withdrew it from the grill. She must do something quick. The young Mexican would not dare hang around too long. Her frantic gaze searched the room. No paper, no pencil. Nothing she could use for a note.

Her heart sank, and was suddenly pounding. The buckle on her hat, a silver thing her father had made for her himself, a tiny replica of his own JC cattle brand.

In a moment she had the buckle in her hand and was back at the iron grill. The young Mexican was still there. She waited for his look, squeezed her arm between the bars and flipped hard. The buckle cleared the balcony rail, disappeared from view.

She withdrew her arm, watched, anxious, hardly daring to breathe. The Mexican seemed maddeningly slow, and she began to fear he had not seen the fall of the buckle.

Relief waved through her. He was moving now, sauntering toward her. He disappeared under the balcony, reappeared, paused again near the fig tree. He turned, took off his steeple hat. Her heart leaped. He was pinning the JC buckle to his hat.

Again his face lifted in a brief glance, his hand made a slight gesture, and then he was turning into the street.

Mary left the window, sat down on the edge of the bed. She felt suddenly limp. The last hours had been a nightmare of horror. For the moment she could not bear to think of them, even dare wonder about her father and King Malory, wonder if the note Garson had sent to the ranch had lured them back to Bar G to certain death.

Garson was so confident they would come, risk any danger to save her. He was right, too dreadfully right. Only they would not find her at Bar G ranch now. It did seem as if the end had come, but while life was in her she would keep on fighting and hoping.

She put her thoughts on the young Mexican. His strange interest in her was more than odd. Some powerful motive had caused him to follow and search her out. His caution told her that he had deliberately taken a great risk, would possibly have been killed if she had been seen throwing him the silver buckle.

The puzzle was too much for her tired mind. She sank back on the bed, closed her eyes and was almost instantly asleep.

CHAPTER
NINETEEN

Raid below the Border

The late moon was well up when King and Sandy left the old Comanchero road and followed the twisting course of a *barranca* that the cowboy said would pass within a hundred yards below Franciso Cota's *cantina*.

"Trail cuts up the slope into the back yard," Sandy said. "Won't nobody see us."

An elderly *mozo* greeted them, suspicion dissolving into a friendly grin as he recognized the blond cowboy. They exchanged polite expressions of mutual pleasure at the meeting.

Sandy slid from his saddle and gestured at King. "A good friend, Pablo," he told the *mozo* in Spanish.

Pablo's grin widened and he gave King a shrewd look that indicated he was under no illusions about the business that usually brought gringos to Los Higos.

King got down from his saddle. "Take good care of the horses," he instructed. He put a gold piece in the *mozo's* palm. "Leave the saddles on."

"*Si.*" Pablo's eyes glistened. This gringo was a fine gentleman. *Un grande caballero.*

They left him, and Sandy led the way across a moonlit patio and through a door and down a wide

218

passage. Another door opened, showed a face, a pair of lustrous dark eyes. King heard an exclamation and the door opened wide and a slim girl rushed into the passage with a flutter of gay-colored full skirts.

"*Sandy mio!*" Her arms went around the cowboy's neck. "*Querido!*" Her soft Spanish was a gurgle of delight.

Sandy gave King a shy glance. "Juanita," he muttered. He pulled the girl's arms down. "Listen," embarrassment made him forget his Spanish, "here's my boss lookin' at us."

The girl drew back, tilted her chin at King. "You 'ave new boss, Sandee?" Her tone was puzzled.

"I've quit Garson's outfit," Sandy said.

Juanita's eyes swept him an approving look. "Uncle Francisco will be glad," she told him in her soft Spanish. She seemed suddenly doubtful, her look again on King.

He shook his head. "I'm not a rustler."

Her laugh tinkled. "Señor!" She made a curtsey. "I am glad Sandy has a new boss like you." She paused, concern suddenly in her eyes. "You are so tired and hungry. Come, I will tell Felipe to prepare food and hot drink."

Sandy held her back, hand on her arm. "Listen, Juanita, some place where folks can't see us. And we ain't got much time." He hesitated, looked at King, added awkwardly, "The boss wants to see Manuel if he's around."

Alarm filled her eyes. "Manuel?" She hesitated. "Why must you see Manuel?"

"He promised to stay here at the *cantina* until I came," King explained.

Juanita looked doubtful. She was thinking of the gold pieces in her brother's pocket. Manuel was in trouble, which would explain his strange behavior that evening, so restless he could not remain still for five minutes and making endless trips down the street and back.

King guessed the reason for the distress on her face. He said, gently, "Manuel and I are good friends. He is working for me."

Her frown lifted. "You gave him the gold pieces?" she asked quickly.

King nodded. "It's important I see him immediately. He may have news for me."

"He is very troubled tonight." Juanita spoke thoughtfully. "Something frightens him, but he does not say what it is that makes him so afraid."

King said grimly. "I think I can guess, Juanita. Please hurry!"

She sped down the passage, opened a door, motioned them to enter. "I will bring Manuel," she whispered, and closed the door.

The room was in darkness. Sandy lit a match, glanced around, saw a candle and put the flame to the wick. The dim light touched King's face, drawn, haggard, the look of a man in the grip of a deadly fear.

The door suddenly opened and Manuel slid into the room. His sister followed, a small coal-oil lamp in her hand. She set it on the table, stood silent, saw Manuel take something from a pocket and hold it out to the grim-eyed Americano.

"Señor," Manuel was breathing hard. "She threw it to me from the window."

The silver buckle lay in King's hand. He gazed at it, a little replica of Jim Carroll's JC cattle brand. He forced himself to speak.

"How long ago, Manuel?"

"The shadows were crawling when the man drove up the street with her. He was the man who used to visit Señor Garson, the one with the waxed mustache, who once tossed me a silver dollar."

"Vince Lestang," muttered Sandy. The cold rage in his eyes made Juanita wonder. She knew Señor Lestang and had thought him a most elegant caballero. It seemed she was wrong.

"She looked at me, and her eyes were very frightened." The young Mexican drew himself up proudly. "I remembered my promise to be your eyes and your ears. I followed them to the house of El Gato."

Juanita smothered a horrified cry. "*Madre de Dios!*"

King stared at the silver buckle in his hand. He understood the reason for the Mexican girl's shocked exclamation.

"You say she threw it to you from a window?" he asked Manuel.

"Si," Manuel related the circumstances. The look on the face of his *amigo* Americano was making him nervous. "I — I could do no more, señor," he faltered.

"You did well," King reassured him. He was again silent, and the others saw from his expression that he wanted no more words.

"Is Lestang still at this El Gato place?" he suddenly asked the Mexican.

"Si, señor."

King's eyes questioned Sandy. "You know this place?"

"Sure do." The cowboy showed embarrassment. "El Gato's a big man in this town. Does plenty business with Garson."

Again King understood. He said, thoughtfully, "There's a chance Lestang hasn't told him about the way you quit your job with Garson."

"It's a good gamble he ain't done any talkin' yet," Sandy agreed. His eyes narrowed. "If you figger for me to do some scoutin' over there, it's all right with me."

"We'll both of us go," King said. His bleak smile was on Juanita. "Heard any talk in this town of an outlaw named King Malory?" he asked her.

Her eyes widened at him. "You?" Her startled look went to Sandy who grinned reassuringly.

"He ain't no outlaw," he said laconically.

"I want El Gato to think I am," King said with another bleak smile. "Fooling El Gato is our one chance to get inside that place tonight, Sandy."

"I'm playin' the hand your way." The cowboy's tone was grim.

King nodded. "We'll wander over there and play the cards the way they fall," he said. "You're known as a Garson man, and that's an ace card we hold to start with."

Sandy grinned. "That's right. With me along won't be nobody lookin' cross-eyed at you too quick."

"We'll play 'em as they fall," King repeated. He turned to the door.

"No, no!" protested Juanita. "You must eat."

King shook his head, passed into the hall. Manuel followed him. "Señor, I go with you."

King hesitated. He could hear Sandy's voice. *Ain't no time to waste eatin'. Got to get that gal away from that place awful quick.* A brief silence, a sound that was unmistakably a kiss, and Sandy was in the hall, breathing a bit too hard, his face flushed.

"I go with you," insisted Manuel. "I know the window."

"All right." King's eyes were warm on him. "Get us out of here quick, Manuel. I don't want anybody to see us."

He took them out by a side door, and after a cautious look up and down the street, they crossed over to the plaza where moonlight laid a soft halo over the ruins of the ancient church. Here and there a lamp glowed from a window. The night was very still. Only the twang of a guitar and a man's voice serenading under some dark balcony.

Manuel's hand lifted in a gesture at the building down the street, the only one ablaze with lights. "El Gato," he said in a whisper.

"Don't need to tell me," muttered Sandy.

"You do not know the window which is upstairs, the third from the corner," reminded the Mexican.

King looked at him thoughtfully. "Do you know where Lestang stabled his team?" he asked.

"Si." Manuel nodded. "In El Gato's big barn." He seemed to understand the purpose of the question, and added, "I know Pedro Mendoza who sleeps there. He is stupid."

"We will have to get away from here fast — if we have good luck." King was thinking aloud. "Might be a good idea to have those Morgan trotters hooked up and all ready to go."

"Si, señor." Manuel's grin was beatific.

"You will tell Pedro Mendoza that Señor Lestang is leaving town at once and wants his team ready."

"He is a stupid one," reiterated Manuel. "He will also be drunk from too much wine by this time. I know that pig."

"Have the buckboard waiting somewhere close," King told him. "We will be in haste."

Manuel thought for a moment. "There are stairs that lead down to a back door. I will wait outside where it is dark under the trees."

"We might see if that back door is locked," suggested Sandy. "We could go up those stairs to get to her room."

Manuel slid away, and Sandy spoke again, his voice doubtful. "Seems like Lestang will make plenty trouble if he spots me. He mebbe ain't told El Gato about me yet, but he'll sure yell out loud quick as he lays eyes on me."

"We'll have to see him first, and alone," King said grimly.

Manuel returned, his expression gloomy. "The back door was locked on the inside," he told them.

"Looks like we go in the front door," Sandy commented. He eased the gun in its holster. "All right, boss."

The man behind the bar was an American, and perhaps he had reason to be wary of strangers from north of the border. Suspicion filled his hard eyes as the new-comer pushed his way through the crowd and got a foot on the brass rail.

King gave him a friendly smile. "What's yours, Sandy?" he asked his companion.

"Most any brand of hootch Dixie Jack can pour into a glass suits me," drawled the cowboy.

The barman's frown faded. He jerked Sandy a recognizing grin, reached promptly for bottle and glasses. "How's things out at Bar G, Sandy?" he inquired genially.

"Fine as silk," glibly assured the cowboy. "Dal says for you to have one on him." He tossed a silver dollar on the bar.

"Sure will," grinned Dixie Jack. He reached for another glass. "Got business in town, feller?" He dropped a sly wink.

Sandy winked back, said softly, "You ain't never met up with Malory, huh, Dixie?"

Whisky splashed from the glass the barman was lifting to his lips. His eyes bulged in a startled look at Sandy's American friend.

"Malory! King Malory!" Excitement made him stutter.

"The same," grinned the cowboy. "King figgers to meet Vince Lestang here. They got a big deal on." He added casually. "I reckon Vince got in, didn't he, Dixie? He said for us to meet him here."

The barman drained his glass, set it down, picked up a cloth, made polishing motions. "Sure he's here. Didn't say nothin' about you fellers comin'."

"Reckon he'll show up," commented Sandy. He slid a look down the long room. A piano player was pounding out a waltz, and some dozen couples were dancing. Other groups crowded the card tables — Mexicans and a sprinkling of hard-faced Americans. Nobody he recognized.

The barman was speaking. "Vince is back in the office right now talkin' with the boss. I can send in word to him."

"No hurry," drawled King.

"Might try your luck at the tables," Dixie suggested. "Faro, monte, poker."

"Poker's my game," grinned King. "Come on, Sandy, let's buy us some chips."

They sauntered away, and King said in a low voice, "That door just off the dance floor is my guess. Couple of girls came in that way."

The cowboy nodded. "Seen 'em go out that way, too. I'm bettin' there's stairs on the other side of that door."

"Take it easy," King warned. "Dixie is watching us. We'll have to mingle a bit, then work around to the door"

The barman's voice suddenly reached them. "Hey, fellers, here's the boss!"

King's heart sank. He was desperately anxious to reach the door to the stairs. The risk was too great. To ignore the barman's summons would invite sure disaster.

El Gato stood stiffly erect by the bar, a short, thick-bodied man with a thatch of coarse, frosted black hair and small, watchful eyes in a brown face pitted with smallpox scars. He looked formidable, this Chihuahuan.

He said, his voice singularly soft coming from so gross a body, "You are look for me, no, señor?"

King answered him in Spanish. "It is a great pleasure to meet one so famous as El Gato, but, no, señor, it is Señor Lestang I came to see."

A hint of a smile relaxed the set mask of the pitted brown face. He clung to his slow-worded English. "You are thees King Malory, no?" His eyes stabbed like rapier points. "I 'ave 'ear of you."

King's answering smile hid his frantic apprehensions. Apparently El Gato was not yet inclined to be suspicious, but any moment might bring Vince Lestang through the office door.

A crowd was drifting up to the long bar, attracted by the *bandido's* presence. A tall, blonde girl pressed against him, a cigarette in red-lipped mouth, her eyes languishing, inviting. El Gato laughed, looked at King.

"She nize, no, thees loafly *Yanqui*. I 'ave new *Yanqui* upstairs. Lestang 'ave go to her now."

The tall blonde dropped her cigarette and threw her arms around the Chihuahuan's neck. "She ain't gettin' you away from me!" She pressed her mouth to his. He laughed, drew her into a tight hug.

It was the distraction they wanted. King and Sandy edged away from the crowding bystanders. The barman paid them no attention. He was too busy.

They slipped through the door, found the stairs and went up quickly, their feet soundless on the thick red carpet

"Manuel said the third door from the end," Sandy whispered when they reached the landing. He gazed up and down the long dimly lit corridor. "Ain't sure which end he meant."

King gestured with his gun. "From the plaza side." He was moving again, soft-footed as a panther. He halted abruptly, lifted a warning hand.

Sandy saw the faint ribbon of light under the door. He made a swift count from the end of the corridor, gave King a grim nod.

King motioned for him to stand close to the wall, rapped softly with his knuckles. A man's voice answered, surprised, impatient.

"Who is it?"

King eyed the doorknob. He feared to touch it, put Lestang on guard. He spoke softly, slurred his words. "Señor, El Gato say coam queek!"

There was a brief silence, an annoyed exclamation, the soft thud of steps on carpet and as the door jerked open King had his foot against it.

Incredulity, a growing horror filled the eyes of the man facing him. He cringed under the press of the gun against his stomach.

King said, his voice a low whisper, "Back up, Lestang."

228

The blood drained from the saloon man's face. He obeyed, lifted his hands. Sandy came in, quietly closed the door and turned the key.

"No talk," warned King. "All right, Sandy, you watch him."

The cowboy leveled his gun. His eyes were bitter, full of deadly promise. Lestang stood rigid.

King was looking at Mary now. She was leaning back against the iron grill, eyes big in her white face. He went to her swiftly, took her into his arms, held her tight for a brief moment.

He made no attempt to talk, saw her hat and gave it to her. She crammed it on, the color back in her cheeks now. He glanced quickly around the room. She shook her head.

"Nothing else mine."

King led her to the door. He opened it, took a look in the corridor, motioned to Sandy.

"The back stairs," he whispered. "Lestang goes first. Let him feel your gun in his back all the way down."

The saloon man stepped into the corridor, Sandy close on his heels, his gun against Lestang's spine. King and Mary followed. They came to another landing and went quietly down a dark stairs.

They reached the door and Sandy forced Lestang to face the wall while King felt for the key. It was in the lock. He turned it gently, swung the door open.

"All right," he said.

Sandy prodded Lestang outside. King closed the door, locked it, threw the key away. Sandy was already hurrying Lestang to the buckboard waiting in the darkness under the trees. Manuel climbed out, stood by the team while King helped Mary into the front seat. She picked up the reins. Her coolness pleased him. No hysterics, no tears. His gaze lingered briefly on the pale blur of her face. She was smiling.

He turned his attention to their prisoner, motioned for him to climb into the back seat.

"We should tie the skunk up," worried Sandy, hand on Lestang's arm, holding him back.

"Later," King said. "We've got to get away from here fast."

"Got me a cord in my pocket," Sandy said. "Long enough to tie his hands." He whipped out a tough piece of twine. King held his gun against the man's head while the cowboy fastened a tight loop around his wrists.

He motioned again with the gun. Lestang climbed awkwardly into the back seat. Sandy followed him, jabbed his gun into the saloon man's ribs.

"One whisper out of you and I'm squeezin' trigger," he warned. "Savvy?"

Lestang said nothing. His face was like chalk under the wide brim of his black Stetson.

King slid into the seat by Mary's side, took the reins from her, and beckoned to Manuel.

"Got another job for you, Manuel," he told the Mexican.

"I will do it," Manuel replied simply.

King hesitated. "Perhaps we can send Pedro."

The Mexican's white teeth glimmered in a grin. "Pedro did not behave, señor. I had to tie him up and hide him in the straw."

"All right, here's the job. Go around front and tell the man at the door that Señor Lestang wants El Gato to know that business has called him back to San Lucas and that he has taken the woman with him."

"Si, señor." Manuel's expression was wistful. "I do not go with you?"

"You bet you go with us." King's hand went out. "You're a man!" His fingers closed hard over the Mexican's slim hand. "Head back to the *cantina* the moment you pass on the message. Our horses are in the barn, saddles on. Put Sandy's roan on a lead rope and fork my Silver King. You'll have to ride fast to overtake these trotters."

"Si, señor." Wind parted the overhead branches and let down moonlight on the young Mexican's face. His smile was something to see.

Mary leaned toward him. "You are a brave man," she told him in a breathless whisper. "You have saved my life."

"Señorita," the young Mexican's gesture was worthy of a caballero, "for a man eet ees not'ing w'at I 'ave do."

The buckboard moved away, left the deep shadows of the trees. King kept the horses down to a walk until they were beyond the ancient church. They passed the *cantina* of Francisco Cota. Sandy, his gun snug against Lestang's quivering ribs, thought regretfully of Juanita. He would never be welcome in Los Higos again, not while El Gato was alive. He would have to send for Juanita in the not too distant future.

The trotters lengthened their stride, and soon they were rocking along the old Comanchero road, the border five miles away.

Mary stirred, looked at the man beside her. "You got my silver buckle?"

His hand closed over hers. "Yes."

She hesitated. "My — my father —"

King said, gently, "He's all right." He squeezed her hand. "We won't talk about it now."

She stole another look at him. His face was stern, almost frightening. His thoughts were on a job still to be done. He had learned much, suspected more. The man on the back seat could tell him things if he could be made to talk. Vince Lestang, who had a habit of secretly visiting Cole Garson, was one of the links in the sinister chain of cattle rustling and murder. He heard Mary's voice again, timid, insistent.

"King, there is something I must tell you."

He looked at her. Her face was pale. "Yes," he said. "Yes, Mary?"

"When I was at Garson's house, before Lestang took me away, I could swear I heard Ed Yate's voice, talking to them." She faltered. "You won't believe me, but it's true."

King said, his voice very quiet. "I do believe you."

Moonlight touched his face, hard, implacable. Mary shivered. This business was not yet finished.

CHAPTER
TWENTY

Rain

Cliff Burl stood straddle-legged in the doorway of his office. His beefy face wore a disgruntled look. Something was wrong and he was helpless to do anything about it. He would like to know why Gil Daly and his Diamond D outfit should be in town so early in the day. Too early for any fun at the Border Palace. The dance hall was never open for business until after dark. As a matter of fact the Daly outfit seldom came to San Lucas on pleasure bent. Deming was Diamond D's town.

The town marshal chewed savagely on his toothpick, spit out the splinters. He resented the way Gil Daly had as good as told him to mind his own business. As if a peace officer had no rights in his own town. He wondered vaguely about Vince Lestang. Mighty queer about Vince. He hadn't showed up in town for over three days.

His morose gaze fastened on a lone rider drifting up the street. His eyes narrowed in a harder look. The man in the saddle was a stranger, but he was reasonably sure he recognized the buckskin horse.

He continued to watch, saw the rider pull up at the hitch rail in front of the San Lucas Hotel where several Diamond D men lounged in the shade of the porch. Their blank faces indicated a complete lack of interest in the stranger.

The town marshal hitched at sagging gun belt and started up the street. The buckskin was a Flying Y horse, and it seemed a good idea to ask the stranger to explain why he was riding him.

The sharp rap of bootheels behind him made the town marshal glance over his shoulder. Ben Wire, moving so fast he was almost running, had his old sheriff's star pinned on his shirt and was wearing his gun. Ben was sure getting loco the way he hung onto his sheriff's star when he wasn't sheriff any more.

Cliff Burl frowned. He'd have to warn Ben he'd get into trouble if he went round flashing that star. He'd toss him in jail for impersonating a law officer. Right now it looked like Ben was going after that stranger.

He slackened his stride, let the liveryman overhaul him. The hard look on the wiry little man's face somewhat disconcerted him. He decided to let the matter of the unlawful star pass for the moment. Old Ben had a hair-trigger temper. It was best to wait until he could catch him without that forty-five in his holster.

The town marshal forced an amiable grin. "Was figgerin' to ask that feller how come he's ridin' Ed Yate's buckskin," he said.

"Might be Ed sold him the bronc," suggested the liveryman.

234

"I'm findin' out." Burl's hand was on his gun now. He halted, feet wide apart, looked the stranger over belligerently. "Where did you get that bronc, mister?" he asked. "Looks like a Flyin' Y bronc to me."

"Any business of yours?" the man finished making the tie-rope fast.

A puzzled look crept into the town marshal's eyes. "Seems like I've seen you someplace, or seen your pitcher." He broke off, hand jerking at gun. "You're that King Malory feller as busted jail the night I was out of town. Get your hands up, mister!"

Horror suddenly bulged the town marshal's eyes. Something hard was pressing against his spine. He stood there, rigid, gun clutched in half-raised hand.

Ben Wire said softly from behind him, "Drop your gun, Cliff."

The town marshal unclasped fingers, let the gun slip to the ground. He managed to get his voice back, said hoarsely, "You cain't do this to me, Ben. I'm a law officer."

"Not any more, you ain't," Ben told him grimly. "I'm throwin' you in jail, Cliff."

"You're loco," yelped the town marshal. "You ain't the sheriff of this county no more. You cain't put me nor nobody in jail." He appealed to the silently interested cowboys lounging on the hotel porch. "You fellers haul this crazy coyote off my back. He thinks he's still sheriff."

One of them grinned derisively. "He's the sheriff all right, mister. We ain't buckin' the sheriff if he wants to throw you in jail."

The town marshal's big body sagged. The thing was too much for his whisky-soaked brain. He only knew that something was very wrong. He heard Ben Wire's voice, a harsh rasp now, "Ed Yate's pet sheriff ain't sheriff no more, Cliff. He's layin' in the Deming jail, charged with aidin' cow thieves and doin' plenty things a sheriff ain't supposed to do." Grim satisfaction touched Ben's voice. "I've been appointed sheriff to fill out his term, and I've sworn in Gil Daly's outfit as posse. We aim to throw a lot more of you skunks in jail."

He seized Burl's dangling hands, jerked them back and snapped on handcuffs. "All right, boys," he said briskly. "Couple of you take him over to jail."

"I want to see Vince Lestang," mumbled the frightened man. "Just as quick as Vince gets in, I want to see him."

"No chance," drawled King. "You'll have to wait a few days, Burl. You see, Lestang is wearing handcuffs himself, right now."

The town marshal stared at him stupidly. "Ain't you the outlaw feller that busted jail?" he stammered.

Amused guffaws came from the hotel porch, and Ben said dryly, "King ain't no outlaw."

Two of the cowboys hustled the prisoner away. Sheriff Ben Wire lifted a beckoning hand. "All right, boys. Let's take a look at the Border Palace and round up some more coyotes." He chuckled. "Cliff ain't goin' to feel lonesome when we get finished combin' out this town. He looked inquiringly at King. "You comin'?"

King shook his head. He had bigger game on his mind. He said, warningly, "Work fast, Ben. No telling when Garson and Yate will get in. Those letters we sent should bring them in a hurry."

"We'll be ready," confidently asserted the sheriff. He clattered away, fierce-eyed, exultant, his posse close on his heels. Their pounding boots made a lot of noise, drew excited faces to doors and windows. An astonished rancher, about to tie up at the hitch rail in front of the saloon, hastily climbed into his seat and drove madly down the street to the livery barn.

Sam Doan came out quickly from the hotel lobby. Gil Daly, a chunky, grizzled-bearded man, followed him, both with guns in their hands.

Sam gave King a grin, glanced down the street. Sheriff Wire and his posse were just disappearing through the swing doors of the Border Palace.

"Looks like Ben's gettin' busy," Sam said. "Didn't know you'd got in, son," he added.

"Only just did," King told him. "Burl was all set to arrest me, and Ben jumped him and rushed him off to the jail."

Gil Daly stared at the road where it curled over the ridge southwest of town. He turned keen eyes on King. "Dust lifting over there," He said laconically.

"That'll be Garson," guessed Sam. He gazed for a moment. "Seems like the whole Bar G outfit is with him from the looks of that dust."

The Diamond D man nodded. "I reckon my boys can handle any bunch Garson brings." He eyed King again.

"Knew your grandfather, young fellow. Never could swallow that story of him being a cow thief."

"He wasn't," King said simply.

"Where's Pete and Sandy?" inquired Sam.

"Back at the Bear Canyon camp with Jim and Mary, keeping an eye on Lestang." King smiled at Gil Daly. "Ben doesn't need them here, not with these Diamond D boys doing posse work for him."

"That's right," chuckled Sam. "Gil's outfit is the toughest bunch in the Territory." He was gazing down street where men were milling outside the doors of the saloon. "Looks like Ben's cleaned the place out," he added as the sheriff appeared, pushing a white-aproned barman in front of him.

King was not much interested just then in the small fry. Nor was he even watching the rapidly approaching dust haze southwest of town. Garson was small fry, too, compared with Ed Yate. The Flying Y man would come from the opposite direction. And he surely would come if Manuel had succeeded in getting the message to him. It was the same message he had sent Garson, with one slight but all-important difference. He had forced Vince Lestang to write both of them. They would recognize his handwriting and have no reason to doubt their authenticity.

Elation burned in him as he thought of the signed confession he had forced from Lestang. The scrambled pieces of the puzzle had at once fallen into their proper places. Staggering, incredible, but true. Garson, the crooked lawyer, the forger, the tool. Ed Yate, the crafty schemer who had hidden the evil he did under a cloak of respectability that for fifteen years he had managed to keep inviolate. It was Ed Yate who had coveted old King Malory's great ranch, planned the shameful deed that had cost him his life and good name. He had lurked in the background, waited for the forged papers to establish Garson as the murdered man's partner and heir. When he finally appeared it was as a newcomer in the San Lucas country. He was safe enough. Garson went through the farce of selling him the major portion of the stolen ranch, was allowed to retain the range on the border as his share of the loot. The little lawyer, grasping, cold-blooded, became his willing colleague in the wholesale cattle rustling that soon began to plague honest San Lucas cowmen. The location of his Bar G ranch on the border made it easy to run cattle across the line where El Gato's vaqueros took over, changed brands, and ran them back for Garson to market.

No man on the Flying Y payroll had reason to suspect the secret activities of their respectable and respected boss. Flying Y skirts were kept scrupulously clean. Ed Yate stood for all that was best in the cattle country.

With fast increasing prosperity he began to look for weak links that might prove his undoing. He worked secretly against the re-election of Sheriff Ben Wire. Ben was too good a sheriff and had an uncanny nose for smelling out rustlers.

He got rid of Sam Doan and Pete Walker. Not because they suspected him, but they had once worked for the man he had murdered.

Another weak link was Cole Garson, now rich and inclined to be too independent; and still another was the disturbing discovery that old King Malory had left a grandson who was making a name for himself in the Texas Panhandle.

Yate's scheme to destroy both Garson and King was grim proof of his crafty brain. The organization of the Stockmen's Association was the framework for a double killing that could never be laid at the Flying Y man's door. King was to have the job as special investigator, pose as a notorious outlaw and gain the confidence of the rustlers. The trail would lead to Cole Garson and the encounter would be almost sure to result in a gun fight fatal to both men. Garson had tried his best but, like Yate, he had underestimated King Malory who had private reasons of his own for wanting to keep the Bar G man alive.

Yate must be a most disappointed man, King reflected grimly. No doubt he had been confident that, at the worst, Garson would put a quick end to the grandson of the man they had murdered. Only another hunted outlaw slain and no man able to point an accusing finger at the head of the Stockmen's Association.

Lestang's story of his own part in the affair was vague. It was King's guess that the saloon man's friendship with El Gato had given him a chance to exert pressure, force the criminals to hand over the Calabasas range as the price of silence.

Lestang, a coward at heart, had babbled out all he knew of the sordid story, a rope around his neck with Pete Walker on the other end, making lurid promises to pull on it if the terrified man held back the truth. The signed confession was a death warrant for Ed Yate and his partner in crime.

Sam Doan's voice drew King's attention to the rider coming up fast from down street. "Looks like Manuel," Sam said.

The Mexican saw the buckskin horse at the hitch rail and reined in quickly. He slid from his saddle and ran stiffly up the porch steps.

"Señor." He wiped his hot, dusty face. "I 'ave geeve heem note." He added in Spanish, "He is the tall gray one who always came in the dark to the rancho."

King nodded. He was not needing confirmation now of Yate's secret visits to Bar G.

Sheriff Wire hurried up, a grin on his leathery face. "Let's get set for that Bar G outfit," he said. "Another ten minutes will see 'em in town."

The activities of the posse had laid a hush on the street. Here and there a horse drooped at a hitch rail. A rancher drove away from the store, a woman under a poke sunbonnet by his side on the wagon seat. Clouds were piling over the mountains, suddenly obscured the sun. The woman dragged off her bonnet, turned a hopeful face up at the darkening sky. There was a promise of rain in those drifting clouds and King found himself thinking of Mary and her father, of JC's dry creeks and springs.

"Got the boys all set?" Gil Daly asked the sheriff.

The sheriff nodded. "Staked out most of 'em in the Border Palace." He chuckled. "Reckon that's where them Bar G fellers will head soon as they hit town." He eyed around thoughtfully at their grim faces. "Sam, you and Gil can set here on the porch, make out you're takin' it easy and talkin' about chances for rain. Don't want Garson to get suspicious. Give him a howdy wave when he rides past so he won't think nothin's wrong." He gave King a nod. "All right, young feller. Let's get over to Burl's office."

King met Manuel's questioning look. "You get inside the hotel and keep out of sight," he said. "We don't want Garson to see you — not yet."

He overtook the sheriff, and in a few moments they were inside the former town marshal's office.

"Do you reckon Garson will come here quick as he gets in?" Ben asked.

"That's what the note told him to do." King was listening to the approaching hoofbeats. "The note said Lestang would be waiting in Burl's office. Garson will be in a big hurry to see Lestang."

"You can stand outside the back door," the sheriff said. "You'll want to hear what he says, huh?"

"That's right." King took a cautious look up the street. "Coming fast," he muttered. "Garson is on that black horse of his. Looks like a buzzard, the way he humps over his saddle. Got Dal Santeen with him, and close on a dozen more of his outfit."

He went quickly to the back door, paused a moment, said anxiously, "Work fast, Ben. We've got to get them out of the way before Yate heads into the street."

Sheriff Wire nodded, settled back in the chair behind the desk, drew his gun and laid it across a knee, fingers clenched over butt.

Dust swirled past and two riders halted at the hitch rail. King, crouched outside the back door, heard Garson's high, piping voice. "I won't need you here, Dal. You get yourself a drink and then see Joe Slocum about those supplies the cook wants ordered."

The screen door squeaked and Garson was suddenly inside the office. He fastened a surprised look on the sheriff leaning drowsily back in the chair behind the desk.

"What are you doing here, Ben? Is Cliff out of town, or sick?"

Ben shook his head. "Cliff's over to the jail with a bunch of fellers," he drawled. "I'm just settin' here for him." He yawned, straightened up. "Somethin' you want, Cole?"

"Had a note from Lestang asking me to meet him here."

"I reckon he'll be along," Ben said. "Might as well take a chair. Long ride in from the ranch."

"Getting too old for saddle work," grumbled the Bar G man. He sat down, rubbed a stiffening knee, looked at Ben solemnly. "Shocking news Vince gave me in his note about that escaped outlaw killing Ed Yate." The hint of elation in his murky eyes failed to match his lugubrious face. "Vince says Ed's boys shot the killer dead." Garson stiffened in his chair. "Sounded like a shot outside —" He broke off, stared with horrified eyes at the gun in Ben's hand.

The sheriff said softly, "Keep mighty still in that chair, Garson, or I'll spill your guts all over this floor."

The sharp rap of a running man's boot heels drew up the planked sidewalk. Dal Santeen jerked the screen door open. He was breathing hard, a gun in his hand.

"Boss, hell's bust loose!" His hoarse voice broke off in a startled gasp, as King pushed in from the back hall. The gun in his hand lifted, belched flame and smoke. He slammed the screen door, ran to his horse and snatched at the tie-rope.

The hastily-flung bullet went over King's head. He reached the screen door a scant moment behind the Bar G foreman. The spring lock had caught. He wrenched it loose and slammed outside. Cole Garson's stunned gaze followed him. He was like a man who had just seen some terrifying spectre from the grave.

King could have killed Santeen as he fled from the door. He wanted him alive. The foreman might prove a valuable witness against Yate and Garson. It seemed that Santeen preferred to fight it out. He whirled his horse into the street, saw two possemen run out of the saloon. He flung a quick shot and one of the Diamond D men staggered, went down on his face.

Sam Doan and Gil Daly were in the street now, barred escape past the hotel. Santeen whirled his horse again and tore past the town marshal's office, gun blazing at King.

King felt the bullet lift his hat. He flung a quick shot, saw Santeen pitch from his saddle.

Several possemen ran up, faces dark with anger. "Come close to killin' Pat Lacey," one of them said.

Sam joined them, his face grim. A glance told King that Gil Daly was attending to his badly hurt cowboy.

244

The Bar G foreman was unconscious, bleeding from a shoulder wound. King said curtly, "Get him to the doc. I'll send Ben out to clear the street. Yate is due any moment."

He hurried back to the marshal's office, gave the sheriff a nod. Ben said, "I savvy," and slammed through the screen door.

King stood there, frowning gaze on Garson, huddled back in his chair. He said quietly, "Lestang has told me the story, Garson. I'd like to swing you from a tree and pull on the rope with my own hands, and it wouldn't be murder."

Garson said nothing. His face was gray, his eyes dead coals under his black hat.

"I'm leaving you to the law," King went on in the same toneless voice. "You and Ed Yate will be hanged by the law, not murdered — the way you murdered my grandfather."

He saw the note in Garson's clenched fingers, smiled grimly. "Good bait, wasn't it, Garson? You were mighty glad to get that note telling you that Yate and I were dead."

Garson's thin lips writhed. He spoke, his voice a croak. "Ed Yate was a fool. He should have killed you while he had you in jail."

"I'm hard to kill." King said laconically.

Sheriff Wire pushed through the screen door, a satisfied look on his face. "Sure trapped me plenty skunks over to the Border Palace. Every last one of 'em a cow thief, which is why they was on the Bar G payroll." He grinned at the frightened old man in the chair. "Come on, Garson, you said you was wantin' to see Cliff Burl. Won't promise you'll see him, but I'll give you the cell next door to his so you can listen to his bad language. Cliff sure can cuss."

He took the prisoner outside, turned him over to a pair of possemen who looked at him with hot, belligerent eyes. This was the boss of the man who badly wounded Pat Lacey.

The sheriff accompanied King up the street toward the hotel. "Wasn't you sayin' Ed Yate was to meet Vince at the Border Palace?" he asked.

"Yate will think so," smiled King. "That's what we put in the note."

"He'll be some puzzled when he finds the door locked," chuckled the sheriff. "Sam and me and Gil will be settin' there on the hotel porch, you somewheres back inside out of sight. Ed will likely ask us if we've seen Vince, or mebbe he'll head over to the store and ask Joe.

"Whatever he does, he's due for a big surprise," King said bleakly.

They had not long to wait. Dust haze drifted on the road north of the livery barn and presently the watchers on the hotel porch could see what was making the dust. A lone rider and coming fast.

King got out of his chair, gave his friends a grim nod and went inside. Willie Logan, busy at the hotel desk, glanced up, then hastily lowered his head. He had never seen so stern and formidable a look on a man's face.

Yate was in the street now, horse moving at a fast walk. He glanced at the town marshal's office, seemed about to pull in there, changed his mind and rode up to the hitch rail in front of the Border Palace. He got down from his saddle and went leisurely to the door of the saloon.

The door refused to swing open at his push. He stepped back, stared at it, tried again, gestured angrily, and started across the street toward the store.

Joe Slocum, in his cubbyhole of a post office, looked up from a handful of letters.

"Nothin' in for you today, Ed," he said.

Yate drew out a handkerchief, wiped his perspiring face. "Seen Vince Lestang around?" he asked.

"Ain't seen Vince for three or four days," the storekeeper told him. He cocked an eye at the window. "Looks like we'll get some rain out of these clouds."

The Flying Y man fidgeted with his handkerchief, pushed it back in his pocket. "Vince sent me a note to meet him at the Border Palace," he said. "The place is locked."

"Got delayed, mebbe," drawled Joe.

"Vince said something about Garson tangling with that outlaw and getting killed," Yate continued. "Seems that Dal Santeen caught Malory in the act and filled him with lead."

"Ain't heard about it, Vince not showing up," the storekeeper said. He shook his head. "Well, well, so old Cole's gone, huh?"

A hard smile flickered across the cattleman's face. "No loss, Joe. I've an idea Garson was mixed up with this cow stealing. Shouldn't be surprised but what he and Malory quarreled over some rustling deal and that started the gunplay." He turned to the door. "Well, tell Vince I was looking for him."

The storekeeper's gaze followed him, a curiously hard gleam in his eyes. He snatched up a gun from his desk and pushed hastily through the wicket gate.

Yate was down the steps and halfway across the street when he saw King. He halted abruptly, then reached for the gun in his holster.

The two gunshots sounded like one. Yate's gun fell from his hand. He made a queer half turn, staggered and sprawled flat on his face.

Sheriff Wire hurried down the steps of the hotel porch, bent over the shuddering body. He straightened up, looked at King, standing feet wide apart close to the opposite sidewalk, gun in lowered hand.

"Never will be more dead," he said laconically.

King said nothing, but stood there like a man turned to stone. His face showed pale under its mask of stubble and dust.

Joe Slocum called out from the platform of his store. "I saw the whole thing, Ben. Yate went for his gun first."

"King gave him the breaks," the sheriff said. "Only King was a lot faster. Never seen a man get his gun out as fast as King did," he added in an awed voice.

"Yate thought King was dead," Joe told the sheriff. "Must have sent him loco when he saw King standing there in the street."

"Sure did." The sheriff's tone was grim. "He knew he'd throwed in his last chip — and lost."

Sam Doan followed King to the barn. Manuel was throwing a saddle on the big palomino.

"Leavin' already, son?" Sam's voice was gentle.

"They'll want to know," King said.

The two men stood there, silent, thoughts busy. The Mexican led the horse out. King climbed into the saddle, reached a hand down to Sam.

"Thanks, old-timer." The hard clasp of his fingers said more than words.

Sam watched until he disappeared in the chaparral. He heaved a long sigh, smiled benignly on the Mexican.

"You fork that buckskin out front," he said. "Follow him, only don't get too close. He's wantin' to be alone for a spell right now."

The trail twisted over the ridge, snaked across the mesa and, as he followed it, King became aware of an odd, warming glow in him. He was riding out of a dark pit into a land of light and promise, the black load of intrigue and death gone forever from his shoulders. His churning thoughts took on coherence. There would be a Circle M ranch again in this San Lucas country. Sam and Pete could have their old jobs if they wanted. Circle M would always be home for those two good friends. And Sandy Wells, future foreman of Circle M. The ranch was Sandy's home, too, and Juanita's and Manuel's.

A drop of rain splashed on his face. Rain! Rain was what Jim Carroll wanted so desperately. Rain to save his ranch, bring back to fullness the dry creeks and springs, make lush the parched range. In the meantime

Jim could have Mesquite Springs to graze his cattle there. Mesquite Springs was Circle M again. No man would dare dispute the claim of old King Malory's grandson.

Thoughts of Mary Carroll began to crowd all other thoughts from his mind. Each bend in the trail meant he was drawing closer to her and, as if sensing his impatience, the horse lengthened his stride.

Mary. To think of her quickened his heart. Her trust had never faltered. Her promise had remained true. He knew that all his plans, everything in life must, and always would include her.

The trail dipped sharply, crossed the dry wash, and suddenly he saw her, standing there, heedless of the increasing rain.

He dropped from the saddle, went toward her, not in haste now, but each step slow, for he wanted to feast his eyes, savor the fine spirit in her.

Of a sudden she was moving toward him, and she saw in his eyes that they had come to the end of the long, dark trail. She saw something else in his eyes, and her own eyes answered back.

She said, simply, "King, the rain!" She lifted her face.

Manuel halted the buckskin quickly, swung back around the bend. He must not be too close at a moment so sacred.

... offers a wide range of books in large print, from
... biography. Any suggestions for books you
would like to see in large print or audio are always
welcome. Please send to the Audio Department at:

ISIS Publishing Limited
7 Centremead
Osney Mead
Oxford OX2 0ES

Other titles are available free of charge from:

Ulverscroft Large Print Books Limited

(Australia)
P.O. Box 314
St Leonards
NSW 1590
Tel: (02) 9436 2522

... th, Anstey
... (0116) 236 4325

(USA)
... Box 20
... Station
NY 14225 1230
Tel: (716) 674 4270

(Canada)
P.O. Box 80038
Burlington
Ontario L7L 6B1
Tel: (905) 637 8734

(New Zealand)
P.O. Box 456
Feilding
Tel: (06) 323 6828

... ISIS complete and unabridged audio books
... available from these offices. Alternatively
... your local library for details of their collection
... large print and unabridged audio books.